A Fearless Rebel

Clan Ross
Book Five

Hildie McQueen

Text by Hildie McQueen
Cover by Dar Albert

Dragonblade Publishing, Inc. is an imprint of Kathryn Le Veque Novels, Inc.
P.O. Box 7968
La Verne CA 91750
ceo@dragonbladepublishing.com

Produced in the United States of America

First Edition December 2020
Trade Paperback Edition

ARE YOU SIGNED UP FOR DRAGONBLADE'S BLOG?

You'll get the latest news and information on exclusive giveaways, exclusive excerpts, coming releases, sales, free books, cover reveals and more.

Check out our complete list of authors, too!

No spam, no junk. That's a promise!

Sign Up Here

www.dragonbladepublishing.com

Dearest Reader;

Thank you for your support of a small press. At Dragonblade Publishing, we strive to bring you the highest quality Historical Romance from the some of the best authors in the business. Without your support, there is no 'us', so we sincerely hope you adore these stories and find some new favorite authors along the way.

Happy Reading!

CEO, Dragonblade Publishing

Additional Dragonblade books by Author Hildie McQueen

Clan Ross Series
A Heartless Laird
A Hardened Warrior
A Hellish Highlander
A Flawed Scotsman
A Fearless Rebel

The Lyon's Den Connected World
The Lyon's Laird

Chapter One

Storm clouds gathered overhead, darkening the surroundings in the thickly wooded forest. The wind blew through the branches, making the leaves flutter sideways as birds called out to others, warning of the storm headed their way.

Keithen Fraser's focus was entirely on the man he was facing. Each of his opponent's movements caused him to make calculations of what his own would be. As furious as he was, it was important not to lose sight of his ultimate goal. To kill each of the men he'd been informed who were responsible for the vicious attack on his childhood friend, Catriona.

The slash of the man's dagger came too close for comfort, just a hairsbreadth away from his throat. Keithen pushed the man back, glad to see him stumble and sway. His opponent bled profusely from his nose and cuts across the upper chest and arm.

The man grinned, pacing side to side, biding his time. "We passed her around, each of us taking turns with the wench. I quite enjoyed watching the men use her, over and over again. When it was my turn, she screamed because I took her from behind. I didn't want to be like the others, ye see," he recounted, his eyes gleaming. He spit blood on the ground. "She was given to us. We only did what came freely."

Fury sent blood pumping against Keithen's eardrums and he lunged forward, swinging his right hand in an attempt to plunge his dagger into the bastard's heart. But the man was prepared for it and manage to block the strike. Still, he was able to cut the bastard's arm and then he was forced to leap backward when the man swung with his own weapon.

The man grimaced but managed to smirk. "I left my mark on her. Next time ye bed her, ye cannot miss my bite mark on her left breast. She was quite a morsel."

Keithen roared with anger. "Ye will pay for it with yer life."

When the man rushed toward him, Keithen defended against the fall of the man's blade with his own. Then with his left hand, he punched the man in the gut. Somehow, his opponent managed to stab him as he bent forward. The stab on Keithen's side wasn't deep. He'd been able to move just in time. But it smarted and made him even more furious.

It began to rain, the drops drumming on the tree leaves in a noisy concerto that, under most circumstances, would be nice to hear. Instead, it meant he would be able to slip away without being seen. First, he had to avenge Catriona's lost honor.

"I will kill ye," Keithen gritted each word out and rushed the man who'd continued bleeding, the bloodstains growing on his tunic.

They rolled over each other on the muddy forest ground. The only witnesses to the struggle were their steeds. Keithen's warhorse reared up when they came near, the animal not liking the situation.

The man swung and hit Keithen square in the jaw, sending him reeling backward until his head collided with a tree. Keithen had to shake his head to gather himself.

"Tis too bad ye did not kill me, Fraser, because my laird will ensure every single one of ye dogs are dead by sunset tomorrow." The man turned and ran to his horse.

Keithen was aware that if he allowed the guard to get to the Mackenzie, what the man spouted was true. So Keithen gave chase. The Mackenzie would declare war on his clan.

Fueled by desperation, Keithen caught up with the man just as he reached the mount and sunk his blade into the man's side.

"Argh!" the man cried out and bent forward grabbing his side. Keithen sliced his blade across the man's neck. His opponent grabbed at the injury with both hands, eyes going wide and mouth falling open. Blood seeped from in between his fingers as he finally fell forward to the ground.

Keithen walked to the man's horse and untied it. The animal's return without its rider would alert them to the bastard's death and deliver a message. They'd know another of their guardsmen had been killed. The volatile Mackenzie would go crazy with fury. As Clan Mackenzie had so many enemies, they'd not be able to place blame on any clan for certain.

Even though it was gratifying to have killed another one of those responsible for attacking a woman from his clan, a part of him felt empty. Nothing he did would bring back the Catriona he'd known most of his life.

He'd gotten names from the man he'd just killed. Obviously, the guard had thought he'd kill Keithen, so he'd bragged about which of his friends had participated in the attack.

Three more. At least by his calculations, that's how many were left. Three had died under his hand, now three more would pay for what they'd done.

GALLANT, HIS WARHORSE, flew across the terrain. There was little the great horse seemed to enjoy more than being allowed free rein to gallop. Putting as much distance as he could between Mackenzie lands and his, Keithen rode to a small farm on Fraser lands.

With each fall of his horse's hooves across the ground, his mind went over what had happened lately between the clans. His family was in peril until they agreed to terms the Mackenzie had set. But with the newly formed alliance between his clan and Clan Ross, they were not as vulnerable as before.

Months earlier, along with his father, they'd met the Mackenzie to discuss a truce. The man had suggested marriage between Keithen and his daughter, Ava. Instantly, Keithen had rebuffed the idea. The last thing he wished for was to become forever linked to the man who'd attacked his clan.

Not only had the man been responsible for the deaths of many of his clanspeople, but he'd terrorized surrounding villages, causing people to flee in fear. Too many had lost everything because of the Mackenzie's avarice.

The last thing Clan Fraser wanted was a family alliance with a man no one respected. The Mackenzie grew in power using his large army without a care to the damage they left in their wake.

Keithen would do whatever he could to never be tied to the Mackenzie. Not only because of his lack of care, but mainly because of him throwing a defenseless Catriona to his guards to do with as they wished.

A small keep came into view. Compared to his father's keep, this one had only one small house, a large stable, and two guards.

A large garden that called to a traveler to stop by and admire it, seemed to invite one to rest.

In a small corral were several goats and pigs. The small adjoining field was neatly plowed. Different vegetable plants formed perfect lines on the slight hill.

Keithen admired the planning of the field from which the cook could harvest different items for daily meals.

A dog and its two pups raced to his horse, the tiny beasts not seeming to care that his horse could easily trample them.

When Keithen dismounted, one of the pups bit his boot. The tiny beast growled and shook its head side-to-side.

The mother dog looked on, her eyes moving up to him as if apologizing for her unruly pup. If he'd not been in pain from the cuts, he would have taken time to greet the dogs, but upon straightening, he felt a bit lightheaded.

"What have ye gotten yerself into, Boy?" his aunt, Matilde, called from the doorway. "Ye're a bloody mess again."

A shrill whistle sounded, and the dogs turned and ran to his uncle, Hamish, who gave Keithen a once over and shook his head. "Ye're going to end up dead one of these days." The older man grabbed Gallant's reins and led the huge beast away.

Knowing he'd be treated to fresh oats and perhaps some carrots, the horse went with him as meek as a mouse.

An animal lover, his uncle enjoyed any time spent with a steed like Gallant.

INSIDE THE HOUSE, Keithen was greeted by the aroma of food and bread. He dared not ask to be fed, as his aunt was already cross with him for, once again, showing up beaten, bloody, and without an explanation.

"Take yer tunic off and come sit over here," Matilde instructed while motioning for a maid to pour water into a bowl. "Just know if yer father or mother ask us about this, we will not lie for ye."

Keithen nodded and winced when she took a wet cloth and began to clean out his wound. "That hurts."

"It should," she replied in a flat tone. "I'm going to have to sew it up."

"The fields look good," Keithen told her. "The garden is beautiful."

"Yer uncle has taken over gardening. We've got a helper now, too. Young lad from the village. He's building a small house for himself and his wife over on the creek's side."

Sometimes, Keithen envied the simple life of the villagers. They lived pretty much as they pleased. Unless, of course, they were attacked by warring lairds.

Matilde was his father's sister, a simple woman who'd married the third born son. Although they were not well off, they lived a good life on land that had been granted to them by his grandfather.

Often as young children, Keithen and his sister, Esme, had spent long days there at the small keep. His aunt and uncle, who'd had a son the same age as Esme, had enjoyed having more children there.

"Where is Jamie?" Keithen asked, referring to his cousin.

"Gone to work for yer uncle across the river. Ye know he never wished to remain here. I am not sure exactly what he does, but he lives at the keep. He came here not too long ago with the guard force," she said, referring to a few months earlier when Clan Mackenzie had attacked Keithen's home. His uncle, John Fraser, laird to a larger clan than his, had sent several hundred warriors to defend them.

"Aye, I remember seeing Jamie then. We didn't have time to speak."

"Perhaps ye should consider going to visit yer uncle for a spell as well. Keep yerself out of trouble. It will kill yer mother if I tell her."

Keithen knew his aunt wouldn't tell her. At least he hoped so. "I am doing what I do to protect someone's honor."

"Does the person need that sort of protection?" his aunt asked. "Sometimes, what the person who is dishonored needs is time to heal and to forget. Seeing more hurt and sorrow will not help them."

LAST MEAL WAS being served when Keithen finally arrived at his home. He'd had to ride Gallant hard to make it back at a time that would not cause too many questions.

He did his best not to stumble to the nearest table, where he settled and instantly began to eat. His aunt had refused to give him more than a drink of ale as punishment for not telling her what he'd been up to. The woman loved him and always saw to his injuries, so he understood her frustration with him.

When someone poked him in the shoulder, Keithen turned to find Broden. Broden was a guard and his close friend. The large man gave him a bland look. "Yer father wishes to speak to ye."

Keithen tore off a piece of bread and shoved it in his mouth and then stood to follow Broden from the room. "Did Father eat already?"

"Nay. He's been in here with the council."

That statement did not bode well. Something was amiss. Hunger and discomfort were immediately forgotten as he entered his father's study.

At once, his father's keen eyes traveled over his face. Although he'd done his best to keep from being struck in the face, the man he'd attacked had hit him in the jaw and temple a couple of times.

"It is kind of ye to join us."

Keithen sat at the table. Broden slid a glass of whisky in front of him, and he looked up to see apprehension in friend's gaze.

One of the council members, a lifelong friend to his father, cleared his throat. "We received a missive from the Mackenzie requesting a date be set for the wedding between ye and his daughter. We must reply this time."

Before Keithen could speak, his father leaned forward. "I am sorry, Son. There is nothing we can do to prolong it."

"We are to give in?" Keithen asked. "Are we to allow this man who is responsible for the deaths of many of our people to be joined permanently to us? I will not do it."

His father got to his feet and Keithen did as well. He was prepared to argue the point until an alternative was figured out.

When their gazes clashed, a cold sweat came over him. Keithen knew that look on his father's face. His father's eyes narrowed. "As yer laird, who ye have vowed fealty and obedience to, I order ye to do as I ask. Ye will marry Ava Mackenzie for the good of our clan."

It was a low blow. His father knew Keithen would never stand against him and disobey a direct order. Like every other member of the guard and family, on bended knee, he'd given his sworn oath to give his life for not only the laird, but also for the good of the clan.

Keithen folded his fingers into a fist and placed his right arm over his chest. "Yes, Laird." Unable to utter the word "Father", he'd preferred to use the title. It wasn't supposed to be like this, that a father would order his own son to marry the daughter of the man responsible for so many deaths of their people.

And yet, upon meeting his father's gaze, he understood the decision had not been made lightly.

"Sit down. We must discuss the wording of the message we will send back. If this marriage is to take place, the Mackenzie must agree to the lass coming to live here. We will travel there for the marriage ceremony along with five hundred guardsmen, which will include the contingent from Clan Ross and my brother, Clan Fraser."

Keithen nodded in agreement. Perhaps this would be a way to enact his revenge. His presence on Mackenzie lands could not be questioned as much if he were married to the laird's daughter.

"For a dowry, I will ask for the lands at the forest that border our own," Keithen said.

There was pride in his father's expression at the comment. "That is very good thinking. Why had it not occurred to us?"

By the time the message was written, it was wordy. The messenger was sent away with instructions to not stop until arriving at Mackenzie Keep.

Although not happy to be marrying, Keithen wondered if the Mackenzie would call off the wedding at his request of land. He hoped it would be something the man would not agree to and therefore make it easier to turn down the marriage offer.

As Keithen walked down a corridor, he slowed outside a door that was partly open. Inside, he heard his mother speaking.

She looked up at seeing him and lifted her finger to her mouth, signaling for him to be quiet.

"I do not wish to leave this room," Catriona's voice sounded vacant, without any emotion.

His mother kept a smile on her face. "A walk in the garden

would be nice. I understand ye not wishing to be around people. Although my experience was not as horrible as yers, I am still nervous when guards are about."

"Very well."

Keithen peeked in through the door when his mother motioned him forward. Catriona stood with her back to him. Her auburn hair cascaded down her back. Although she was looking outside and he couldn't see her face, he knew her eyes to be a striking amber brown and her sweet freckled face, once cute, was now astonishingly lovely.

They'd grown up together. For as long as he could remember, Catriona had been part of his life. Of the three, Esme, Catriona and him, she'd always been the more sensible, keeping them in line when they were about to get into troubling situations.

"Mother, I wished to come and greet ye and Catriona." Keithen kept his voice calm, hoping to not startle Catriona.

She whirled around, eyes rounded, mouth open. Her gaze moved to his face only for a split second before she once again turned away, seeming as if she wished to disappear.

"How fare ye, Catriona?" Keithen asked in as soft a voice as he could muster.

Moments passed without a reply. "I am well."

It was a lie, but the reply alone was much more than he'd gotten since her attack. Just recently, she'd began to speak to him, only a word here or there. For the most part, it was obvious she didn't wish to see him or any other man for that matter.

"I am glad to hear it." He looked to his mother, who stood and went to Catriona's side. "Now, off for a walk we go. Ye promised me. The gardens will be empty."

Knowing Catriona did not wish him to accompany them, Keithen walked out. It was good that Catriona would leave the room. He hoped it was the beginning of her healing.

After their experience, his mother and Catriona would share the horrible bond of being taken by an enemy clan.

Although both women had been released when his father and a large army had ridden out to demand it, it was obvious by their appearances that his mother had been treated well. As a laird's wife, she'd been kept in plush accommodations and had been invited to join the family for meals. All the while, Catriona had been handed over to the guards to do with her as they pleased.

Other than not killing her, no boundaries had been set.

Now the once vibrant woman was an empty shell. The hollowness in her eyes showed just how little was left. Catriona was forever changed and the only thing Keithen could think to do was to avenge what had happened.

HE WENT TO the kitchen and asked to be served a bowl of whatever was left over.

"Ye will have a good meal," Eileen, the head cook, pronounced, and immediately ordered the kitchen maid to cook something quickly. Within minutes, he had a plate of meat and stewed carrots along with bread and a tankard of ale.

Although hungry, he barely tasted the food. He needed nourishment for his vengeance plan to continue. Every time he saw Catriona, the need to find those responsible for what had happened grew stronger.

No matter if he ended up dead in the end, the men would pay for what they had done.

His mother entered the kitchen just moments later and asked the cook for warm porridge for Catriona and then lowered to sit across from him.

"She didn't wish to remain outside for long. I have been unable to persuade her to spend more than a few moments out of her chamber. Thankfully, Flora will return tomorrow, and she is especially patient and good with her."

His sister, Esme, had hired a woman from the village, whose husband had been killed in the Mackenzie attack, to be a caregiver for Catriona.

As he listened, he realized his mother probably felt guilty for the difference in the way she and Catriona had been treated.

"Mother, did ye ask them to bring Catriona to stay inside with ye?"

Lady Fraser nodded. "Over and again. I pleaded for it. I told the Mackenzie that she was family. I thought perhaps they kept her in another part of the house, locked in a room. I never once suspected that she was in the dungeon. Poor child." Her voice cracked. "And now that man expects us to accept his daughter in our own home?"

Keithen wasn't aware his mother knew of the decision. Then again, it made sense that his father would have informed her.

"I am not sure how I will ever accept a Mackenzie as yer wife," his mother pronounced.

CHAPTER TWO

THE SILENCE OF the forest filled Ava Mackenzie with peace. Throughout her life, it was the one place she could run away to and be alone with her thoughts. Away from the constant scrutiny of others, she didn't have to worry about saying or doing something that would be cause for scolding or worse by her father.

Absently, she rubbed her upper left arm and winced. Under her sleeve, the arm was purpled from the tight grip of her father's hand the night before. This time, he'd been especially annoyed at her for not participating in hosting a visiting laird and his wife. In truth, she'd forgotten. So many people came and went without fanfare. Most visited out of fear and a wish to remain in Laird Mackenzie's good graces.

The events hosted at Mackenzie Keep were never enjoyable. Every minute slogged by as people fought to feign interest.

Every so often, her parents would host an awkward affair. The meals would consist of stunted conversations and constant grandstanding by her father. To make it even worse, he acted as if every dish presented should astound the visitors.

It was sickening, and despite the bruising, she was glad to have missed the entire affair. Now, the visiting laird was gone and the keep was quiet. Her father had pronounced it to be a good day to hunt and had left with a group of men.

Why he hunted remained a mystery to Ava. Her father had to be extremely careful of who he chose as any of the men could kill him and call it an accident. If they all collaborated, there would be no refuting it. Despite the danger, her father preferred to come across as brave and well-liked.

He often claimed that many clansmen asked to go on the hunts and it was hard to pick who to allow each time. The lie was obvious as he seemed to take the same four men.

The hunting party was usually flanked by twenty or more guardsmen, which meant they rarely caught a boar. If anything, the scouts who were sent ahead to begin the search for the beast were probably the ones who either killed the animal or maimed it so that her father could deal the death blow.

Sounds like that of a horse startled her and she scanned the surroundings but saw no one. Once again, there was a nicker, and she leaned forward atop her own mount to look. She'd purposely gone in the opposite direction of where her father and his entourage had gone, so she didn't suspect it was them.

She pulled her horse to a stop and listened intently. Once again, she heard the sound like that of an animal in distress. With a short sword in her right hand, Ava urged her mount in the direction of the sound. Moments later, she found the source of the noise. A horse's reins had been caught on a low tree branch in such a way that the animal could not get loose.

Upon dismounting, she approached the animal, speaking softly to it while stroking its nose. The horse seemed to realize she'd help, so other than a few snorts of complaint, it calmed.

"There now, why are ye here alone? Where is yer master?" Ava whispered while tugging at the tangled reins. When it became clear she'd not be able to untie the reins, she used her short dagger to cut them loose from the thorny bush.

Once the animal was able to move away from the tree, it took several steps backward but did not flee. It was a tamed horse. By the looks of it, the horse had been well taken care of. Since the animal was on Mackenzie land, she figured it belonged to one of the guardsmen or was one of her own father's stable horses.

She searched the area for a few moments but didn't see anyone about. As much as she wanted to call out, at the same time, it was dangerous to call attention in case someone had attacked the horse's rider and remained nearby.

There was the possibility of danger, which meant she'd have to cut her ride short. Ava grabbed the freed horse's reins and tugged the animal closer to her own.

Since she'd cut the reins, it was not possible to tether the horse to hers. Instead, she held the longer cut portion of the reins so she could bring the horse back to Mackenzie Keep.

As soon as she passed the gates, several guards hurried to her. One of the guards eyed the horse and then looked to her. Her brother, Alastair, hurried forward and glared up at her.

Ava cringed. Her brother would not hesitate to inform her father that she'd been out alone, and she'd be punished.

"Where did ye find that horse?"

She considered not telling him as it would divulge her favorite place to ride and get away. But when he yanked her from the horse and shook her, she decided to comply. "In the woods, just south."

Alastair's upper lip curled. "Who were ye there to meet?"

"No one. I went to be alone."

"With Father's permission?"

"Of course," Ava lied, meeting his gaze. "I did not see anyone injured or about. But I did not call out. The horse's reins had become entangled in low thorny branches."

She hoped that by directing the conversation away from his question, he would not realize she'd lied about having permission.

Without another word, Alastair turned on his heel and hurried to where several guards stood. "Ten guards mount at once," he directed, pointing to her. "My sister will show us where she found the horse."

"Ye recognize the horse then?" Ava asked her brother, who gave her an annoyed look.

"Aye, of course. He is one of our warhorses."

"Who would have ridden it?"

Her brother studied her for a moment. "Perhaps who ye went to meet with."

Not wishing to continue arguing, Ava returned to her horse and mounted.

IT WASN'T LONG before they reached the area where she'd found the horse. The guards dismounted and began searching the area. It was less than an hour later when one called out, and everyone scrambled to the spot.

On the ground lay a Mackenzie guard that Ava recognized. The man was cruel. That much, she knew about him, so she'd had done her best to avoid him. Whoever had killed him had cut the man several times from all the bloodstains on his tunic.

"It's obvious there was a fight of some kind," one of the men said.

"Probably an angry husband," another added, and they laughed.

"Or an intruder," someone else said. "A poacher or trespasser."

"Do any of ye know why he would be out here? Could it be he was a spy, a traitor?" her brother, who always seemed to look for the worst in people, asked.

No one replied. Instead, they looked at one another. Of course, they would not give an opinion as it could possibly paint them as part of a conspiracy.

The dead man was thrown over the back of a horse, and the group split. Two men rode back to the keep while the rest would stay behind and search for clues.

Ava had dismounted and she guided her horse to a creek to

drink. Her brother came up behind her. "Go back to the keep."

"I will," she snapped, not in the mood for his continuing attempt to intimidate her.

He sized her up. "Why were ye really here?"

"Because I like it." She motioned to the surroundings. "It's peaceful and beautiful. There is rarely anyone here as they'd have to cross a long distance through our lands to reach this point."

"Whoever killed Graham made it this far," Alastair pointed out.

Ava lifted a brow. "Then perhaps the killer is one of our own."

For a brief moment, his eyes lowered to the short sword at her waist. "I suppose ye could be right."

When her brother turned away, Ava lifted her foot. Beneath her boot was a dagger that had been partially buried in the soft mud of the creek bank. She recognized the insignia.

A stag, with the words, "Je Suis Prest".

The Fraser crest.

Quickly, she stuck it into a hidden pocket in her serviceable skirts and hurried to mount her horse. Was it possible that it was indeed a Fraser who was killing their guardsmen?

Mind awhirl, she rode back to the keep. There had to be a way to speak to a Fraser and warn them that if whoever it was continued to do this, her father would not touch his heart in retaliation.

He'd send the entire warrior force to decimate the Fraser Clan, without regard for what the aftereffects would be. It would mean years of war against the larger Fraser Clans and anyone affiliated with them.

Ava felt physically ill. She grew increasingly tired of the constant chaos that was her life. If only she would have been married off to a man who was strong enough to take her away from her father's lands.

Instead, her late husband had been weak and too eager to please the Mackenzie. He'd forsaken his own lands and people to move to Mackenzie Keep. The decision had ultimately caused his demise.

WHEN A PAIR of deer appeared just in front of her, Ava froze, watching them. After seeing her, the duo disappeared into the woods.

Ava watched as they vanished, envious of their freedom.

"THERE YE ARE." Her mother stood just inside the great room when Ava returned home. Her face was a study of consternation. "What have ye done now? Yer father is most upset by yer actions."

Ava spoke in a sing-song voice as if reciting a beautiful poem. "I forgot about our visitors and was not there to help entertain them. He's already threatened me with the worst punishment, to send me to a nunnery to live my days, in prayer, in fasting, days and nights upon my knees."

Her mother frowned. "Why do ye say it like so?"

"Perhaps because life in a church sounds appealing."

Lady Mackenzie didn't reply. Her mother would never understand. As hard of heart as her father and brother, her mother rarely showed caring.

Ava often wondered why she didn't have the same disposition as they did. It certainly would help deal with the many unfair things her father had done through the years.

"Come along, dear. We must discuss yer trousseau."

"For what, Mother?"

"As ye well know and insist on ignoring, ye will be married as soon as yer mourning is over."

Ava looked down at her dark clothes. Since her husband's death, she'd grown fond of wearing the nondescript colors. Wearing clothing that fit loosely and unflattering had allowed her more freedom to move about, practice archery and ride.

"What about a pale blue?" her mother was asking. Ava wasn't

sure what she was referring to.

Ava attempted a calm smile. "I do not plan to get married, Mother. Like my late husband, this poor man will end up dead as soon as he disagrees with Father about anything."

Her mother straightened and pinned her with an annoyed look. "Do not add kindling to the fire. Ye should be the first to stand up and deny any rumor that, in any way, yer father had anything to do with Gilbert's death."

"Gillian," Ava corrected.

"Yes, right." Her mother let out a sigh. "I could never remember his name. It must have been a sign. I will do my best to memorize this one's name. Keithen, isn't it?"

At the name, a current traveled down her spine, and she remembered the handsome young man. "I am not marrying. I do not wish to be a widow twice."

"Enough!" her mother exclaimed and motioned for her to follow. "I had the maid bring out some of yer more colorful gowns. Ye will not wear any more of those dreadful rags ye insist on donning."

"My husband has not been dead a year as yet," Ava complained. In truth, she did not have any desire to wear anything colorful or have her hair brushed into complicated styles. The less attractive she looked, the longer she could remain unattached. Her father, for the most part, had let her be since Gillian's death. It was only as of late, in the last couple months, that he'd decided to marry her off for whatever gain he planned.

There was no doubt in her mind that the marriage was planned in order for her father to further grow the amount of land he was laird over. He wanted the Fraser land, and the marriage was his first step toward getting it.

They entered her mother's sitting room to find it transformed into a dressmaker's shop. The array of colorful clothing on display made Ava flinch. Everywhere her eyes landed, there were gowns and shawls of every color imaginable. Never in her life had she seen so many ruffles. The display included garish flower hair adornments, gloves and slippers.

"Ye do realize we live in the Highlands and these clothes are absolutely useless to wear?" Ava motioned to the hair clips. "It seems fashion has changed quite a bit since I last wore color. The last I heard, no one wears feathers anymore."

Her mother narrowed her eyes. "Where would ye hear such a thing?"

"When the Grants were here. Do ye not remember how Lady Grant and her daughters wore their hair in ribbon-wrapped plaits? They wore muted tones of green and amber and only a simple cross on a leather ribbon around their necks."

"They are certainly not someone I would take any kind of fashion advice from!" Her mother shivered. "It was hard not to laugh at the ridiculous hairstyles."

Ava had to admit the plaits weren't at all flattering on any of them. However, the hair ornaments that looked as if they'd been pulled from a very disturbed bird wouldn't be any better.

"Where did ye find this, Mother?"

Lady Mackenzie straightened. "I suppose ye don't remember as ye insisted on staying next to yer husband's deathbed. Yer aunt and uncle visited, and my sister brought them from her travels to India. Or was it England?" As her mother concentrated, Ava lifted one of the adornments.

"I do not believe a bird exists that has these feathers. They must be dyed."

"Ye do not have to wear the feathers, but I would like to see ye in something different for dinner. We have visitors coming any day now."

It would do little good to argue. Instead, Ava nodded, studied the display and decided on a gown that was a pale green. "This one."

THE FAMILY DINNER table had eight chairs. Two remained empty. Across from Ava sat her brother and a member of her father's council, an older man who had an annoying habit of talking with his mouth full. The seat next to Ava remained empty. Her parents sat on opposite ends. Her grandmother, who was visiting, sat at her father's left. The only sounds for a long time were the sounds of food plates moving as they served themselves.

"I am told ye found Graham," her father said, looking directly at Ava. "How is it that ye were out there?"

Her blood ran cold. If her father decided to lock her up until the marriage, she would not be able to sneak away and ride.

"I was practicing at archery and went in search of lost arrows," Ava replied with a practiced, even voice. "I did not find him. One of the guards did. I found the horse."

Her father looked to Alastair. "Was there nothing left in the area to show who did it?"

Alastair shook his head. "Whoever it was had to have been hurt. Graham's knife had blood on it."

"It could have been his own."

The men continue discussing the dead man's injuries, not noticing that Ava and her mother stopped eating at the graphic descriptions.

"He couldn't have been dead that long if ye found him in one piece," her father said as he chewed.

Alastair nodded. "True. No more than half a day I would say."

"Could this conversation not be at the dinner table?" her mother finally spoke up. "It is most unpleasant."

Although her father was a cruel man, he always seemed to soften when speaking to his wife. It could be that, in her own way, her mother was harder than he was. "Of course."

"We must speak of the marriage. Have ye heard back from Laird Fraser?"

Her father looked to Ava. "A messenger just arrived today. I meant to discuss it with ye both. But now that I am learning of our daughter's inability to follow simple rules, I am not sure how to proceed."

"I do not wish to marry." Ava didn't look at anyone at the

table. "I prefer to remain here and not be sent away."

Her grandmother snorted, and everyone turned to find the old woman had fallen asleep. "Get my mother to her chamber," her father said as he motioned a maid over. "Now."

The old woman slapped at the maid. "Get away from me. I have not finished my meal."

"Yes, ye have, Mother," her father said. "They are bringing ye honeyed mead to yer chamber."

Her grandmother lit up. "Then I must go at once." The woman had to have help standing and then to walk out at an excruciatingly slow pace.

The family continued eating in silence for a long time. Finally, her mother brought the subject up again. "What did the message state?"

"They listed ridiculous stipulations," her father said, waving his hand dismissively, "but agreed in the end to the marriage."

Ava's heart sank. "What stipulations?"

"That ye go live there at Fraser Keep, which was my idea, of course. Secondly, that I grant them some border lands as yer dowry." Her father chuckled. "That land is not worth anything, but I suppose it can be hunted on."

"What do we have to gain from it?" her mother asked. "It seems to me they are the ones who hold the upper hand."

"A spy," her father said. "We gain someone inside that will give me all the information I need to not only take over their clan, but also find out who their allies are."

Ava didn't have to ask who the spy was. Her father would expect her to report to him regularly. No doubt, someone would be sent along with her who would take messages back and forth.

When her mother's lips curved, Ava wanted to get sick.

"I wonder if there are families that celebrate marriage for the sake of it. A celebration of love and caring." Everyone either glared or shook their heads as if she were daft.

CHAPTER THREE

FROM ATOP THE wall that surrounded the keep, Keithen scanned the surrounding lands. To the left, there were familiar wooded forests as far as the eye could see. When he looked straight ahead, there was a valley with a road leading to a large village. The air smelled of peat and moistness from the early morning drizzle. The haze was finally lifting aided by a light breeze.

Autumn brought with it cooler weather and rain. Although at the moment, it was quite pleasant.

A cart appeared on the road, heading toward the keep. It was probably one of the villagers bringing sundries for the kitchen. Keithen watched for a long moment before turning and walking to the northern corner of the wall. That area below was almost unreachable on foot, unless one was familiar with the hidden paths that only those who lived at the keep had memorized.

He grunted in annoyance at recalling that someone had shared information about those paths. It was the only explanation because when they'd sent his mother and Catriona to safety during the Mackenzie attack along the hidden paths, they'd been discovered.

Two mistakes had been made that day. The first was sending

young guards to escort them and the second was not knowing they'd been betrayed by their own village constable. The man was dead now, killed by a Mackenzie guard. That had been anticlimactic, as Keithen had wished to be the one to deal the death blow.

"Horseman," Broden called down from atop the roof. The man pointed to the edge of the forest.

"Probably the messenger with Mackenzie's reply," Keithen called back. By now, several archers had lined up and guards rushed atop the gates, everyone with a watchful eye in case others followed the man. As per their training, at the same time, guards and archers were alerted on the southern, eastern and western sides to be alert in case the rider was a distraction of some sort.

The man arrived at the gates and spoke to the warriors who stopped him. They allowed him in.

Keithen rushed to a narrow staircase and hurried down so he could be the first to greet the messenger.

"Whose message do ye bring?"

The messenger was young, but broad of shoulder and with a proud stance. He sized Keithen up. "Who are ye?"

"I am the laird's son." Keithen purposely didn't give his name. "Identify yerself."

"As I told the guards, I come from the Mackenzie with a message for Laird Fraser," the man replied with a flat tone, his distaste evident in the curl of his upper lip. "Will ye take me to yer father?"

If the circumstances had been different, Keithen would punch the man in the face. He wondered if perhaps the man been there when Catriona was attacked.

The Mackenzies considered themselves better than everyone else when, in actuality, in Keithen's opinion, they were nothing more than pack dogs who attacked the vulnerable and weak.

Keithen turned on his heel and walked to the front of the house. Once there, he held out a hand. "Wait here."

He wasn't about to allow the idiot in unless he was sure Catriona was nowhere in sight. His fears were realized when she was, indeed, sitting at a table with her mother, Lady Fraser and the caregiver, Flora.

At noting his father standing next to the hearth speaking with an older member of the council, Keithen neared. "A messenger from the Mackenzie has arrived."

His father looked around him. "Where is he?"

"At the entrance. I wasn't sure about him entering with Mother and Catriona here in the great room."

His father nodded in understanding. His gaze moved to where the women sat, seeming to be chatting about inconsequential topics. Like the rest of the family, his father had a soft spot for Catriona.

Just then, the women stood. Keithen hurried over, noticing immediately that Catriona looked away. "Where are ye going, Mother?"

"To the gardens, for a wee walk," his mother replied with a smile. They would have to go straight out the front door to where the messenger was waiting.

Keithen nodded and hurried to get the man and move him away from their path.

He emerged and motioned the messenger to come with him to the kitchen entrance. Thankfully, the man followed without hesitation. Once inside the keep, he guided the man across the great room and to his father's study.

When they passed the front entrance where the messenger had just been waiting, the man looked to Keithen in question.

"I would ask, but I suppose ye will not tell me why I was granted a tour of the keep."

Keithen ignored him.

They entered the study, but his father was not there. Keithen knew it was done purposely to give the messenger a sense that his visit was not seen as important. This was done in hopes that the messenger would let the Mackenzie know that he was not seen right away.

A maid entered and stood by the doorway to await any order for food or drink. Keithen looked to the young woman, who looked nervous.

The messenger slid a glance to the woman as well and for a just a split second there was a flicker of either recognition or admiration in the man's eyes.

"Gilly, bring our guest something to eat and ale."

"I prefer to give my message and leave," the messenger said.

"Very well," Keithen said and nodded at the maid. "Thank ye, Gilly, ye may go."

"I'd like ale," the messenger then said, seeming to realize Gilly would not return otherwise.

When the maid left to seek the beverage, Keithen met the man's gaze. "Were ye there when my mother and the other woman were taken to Mackenzie Keep by force?"

The messenger looked at him for a long moment seeming to try to find a way to respond. "Aye, I saw them."

"Did ye have anything to do with the attack on the younger woman?"

"I do not have to reply to yer inquisition, but I will. I do not take women by force." The man's face turned to stone, letting Keithen know he'd not answer any further questions.

At that point, his father entered and walked to stand at the front of the room. He didn't pay the messenger much heed.

The laird didn't speak, other than to greet Gilly when she returned with the ale, placed it on the table, and hurried out, not once looking at the messenger.

"What brings ye?" his father finally asked.

The messenger proffered a rolled parchment. "My laird asks that I return with haste with a reply."

His father accepted the parchment and motioned for the man to sit. "I will return momentarily. Remain here."

Keithen followed his father out to the courtyard where another guard was dispatched to find the councilmen and bring them. "Father, how long are ye going to leave that man in yer study?"

His father lifted and lowered a shoulder. The courtyard was bustling with activity. It was early in the day and there were chores to be completed. The clan prepared for a harvest festival that would take place in a few days. They would roast pigs, have music and celebrate the end of the harvesting. It was one of the last times people would travel from afar to participate since the winter weather would make it very hard.

A woman hurried by with a bucket in each hand, a toddler struggling to keep up. Keithen went to her and took one of the buckets. "Why are ye carrying so much?"

"My husband hurt his back," she replied, winded. "I have to help where I can."

"The blacksmith?" Keithen asked, recognizing her. "Is he here?"

When they got to the front side of the stables where a red-faced blacksmith worked, the toddler was screeching, tears flowing down its dirty face. The woman was crying because she thought that Keithen was about to scold her husband and Keithen was exasperated.

He placed the bucket down and searched out the stable master. Together, they went back to the blacksmith, who watched over his fretful wife and child.

"If ye are aware the blacksmith has injured his back, why is he working?" Keithen asked the stable master.

"With the harvest celebration, we will fall behind in work…" The man looked properly chastised and glared at the blacksmith. "Why didn't ye tell me about yer back?"

Moments later, the family rolled out the front gates, the smiling wife guiding the horse toward home, where the blacksmith had been ordered to rest for a week.

"I beg yer pardon, Keithen. I was not aware. I've been busy with the new horses." The stable master shook his head. "He's a hard worker and he's scared to lose his standing here at the keep."

"I will see that someone goes to see them with food and an assurance that his job is secure."

For a long moment, he remained rooted to the spot next to the corral. He had no wish to know what the message was.

He doubted the Mackenzie would cancel the marriage between him and his daughter, Ava. It had been the man himself who'd suggested it, after all.

"Do ye wish to know the reply?" His father had neared. "He agreed to all our terms."

"What is he after? Why would he offer his daughter in marriage to a small clan who doesn't wish for an alliance?"

His father pondered that for a moment. "I believe he is attempting to quell the rumors that he had the young woman's husband killed by sending her away here to us. At the same time, by letting it be known that it was his idea to allow the marriage, he will make it seem as if he's now providing support for us through an alliance."

Rage threatened to erupt outwardly, so Keithen took several breaths. "It will be an alliance, Father. If I marry that woman, we will be allied to our worst enemy."

"If it will save lives from being overrun by him, then it must be done."

"However?" Keithen asked. "There is something bothering ye isn't there?"

At that moment, the messenger emerged from the doorway and looked around. He was flanked by their guards, so he'd probably asked for fresh air. Nonetheless, Keithen kept an eye on the man. If the messenger went anywhere near the young maid, Gilly, he'd put a stop to it.

His father would not send a reply until he spoke with the council. This was a fact they were not obliged to share with the messenger.

"However," his father said. "I am reluctant in that an alliance could mean the Mackenzie decides to absorb us into his clan. How we'd stop it, if it happens over time, I am not sure."

"Dissolve the agreement. We are allied to Clan Ross, our larger clan relatives and perhaps we can meet again with the Grant."

At his father's head shake, Keithen wanted to scream in frustration. "This will not end well, Father. The Mackenzie does nothing without a scheme to overtake and gain power."

"We will deal with it when it comes. I will never allow our clan to fall under any other. There is another way that I have been considering."

Keithen didn't care to remain to hear the talks between his father and the council. Instead, he stalked into the house.

He entered through the kitchen and caught Gilly by herself. She had been peering out the window, her eyes widening when she saw he'd entered.

"How do ye know the messenger?"

Her face turned bright pink, her cheeks reddening. "He was someone I cared for. We met secretly when we were both but a lad and a wee lass. Five years ago. This is the first time I have seen him since the day he promised to meet and did not show."

"Remain away from him." Although Keithen understood young love, he doubted anything good would come between the slight lass and the man who'd brought a message from the Mackenzie.

"I will," Gilly replied with conviction. "Do not worry." Despite the conviction of the words, there was vulnerability in her gaze.

A part of him wanted to reassure her that if things were to be, nothing would stop it. Instead, he nodded and walked away. He went directly to Catriona's chamber. He knocked on the door and Flora, her caretaker, opened the door. Her eyes widened at seeing him.

"I must speak to Catriona," he said.

Flora nodded and stepped back to allow him in. Catriona sat in a chair, her face turned to the window. Obviously, she'd heard him, so she was aware he entered. But outwardly, there was no sign of it.

He lowered to a chair opposite hers and looked to Flora. "Can ye give us privacy, please?"

"Of course. I will fetch something to drink, Catriona," Flora replied and left.

Keithen studied the room for a moment. It was a space suitable for guests with an ornate bed, several tables, an upholstered pair of chairs, and a fireplace that currently did not have a fire burning in the hearth.

"Would ye like me to start a fire?"

Catriona shook her head. "I prefer it cool."

At least she'd finally begun speaking to him, although most of the time it was no more than a word or a short sentence.

"I went to the forest the night before last. I killed another of them," he informed her. "Just three more are left."

Her hand fluttered to her chest. "Ye should not do it again. I do not wish ye to be injured or die because of it." Despite her words, he noted she sat straighter. "I would never forgive myself if something bad happens to ye. Tis best ye stop."

"I cannot." He reached for her hand, but she moved it away. "Understand me, Cat. Ye are like a sister to me. I could never allow them to get away with attacking either ye or Esme in such a manner."

"Do not hurt her, the daughter, Ava. She was kind. Saved me. Although at times, I am not sure I wish it was so."

Keithen's stomach clenched at realizing that if he married the Mackenzie's daughter, Ava and Catriona would meet again. "Ye know I would never hurt a woman."

She lifted her gaze to him and shook her head. "Ye must understand that it matters not what ye do, I will never be who I was again."

"I have hope," he replied. "I know ye will. Mayhap knowing the men who dared to touch ye are dead is the way."

They sat in silence for a moment. Keithen wondered what she did all day. How she could bear to remain in the bedchamber day after day when, before, she'd been so involved in many activities.

"Will ye sit with me at the high board for last meal?"

For the first time in many days, her gaze lifted to his. It was brief, but enough to remember the beautiful amber brown. "No, I cannot possibly sit there."

"I will find ye where ye sit then," he quipped. "Even if it is here."

She sighed. "Ye must understand that who I was, I will never be again."

Of course, over time, he expected that she'd come around. Perhaps as she stated, she'd never be the same. But hopefully, she would not be this recluse, so empty and pitiful.

"I best go see about my duties." Without thinking, he leaned over to press a kiss to her hair. Catriona jumped from the chair and scrambled onto the floor. On all fours, she scurried away and rolled into a ball, her face pressed to the corner where the walls met. Strange mewling sounds came from her, and she began shaking.

Flora rushed in and gave Keithen a sympathetic look. "She will be well in a few moments." The woman went to Catriona and hovered over her, not touching. "Miss Catriona, ye must get up. I fetched honeyed mead, yer favorite."

After a few moments, Catriona lifted her head and looked around as if expecting the surroundings had changed. Upon seeing him, her face turned bright red, and a sob escaped.

"Drink yer mead, it will help," Keithen said. "Forgive me…" he stopped midsentence, not sure what else to say. It didn't seem to matter since Catriona was now standing and looking out the window, effectively dismissing him.

LATER THAT NIGHT, the moon was high as he rode north. Gallant's huge hooves kicked up caked, muddy ground as they traveled across the land, toward the forest where he hoped to be able to slip past any sentinels and into Mackenzie lands.

Now more than ever, he had to find the last three. Once he was married, he would not be able to slip away as easily.

He slowed and left Gallant tethered then continued on foot. Once he arrived at a specific spot, he lowered to sit, leaning back against a tree.

It was almost morning when sounds in the woods woke him. He'd found it easy to hunt down the first three guards as they traveled through that area often in search of entertainment from women who lived just inside the woods. The women served the guards for payment, which came in handy as the men often traveled alone after their shift which meant they were distracted and tired.

He was not disappointed when soon after he'd found a hiding place, a man appeared. He exited the woman's hut and headed in the direction where Keithen was hiding. The darkness made it hard to see if it was the man he sought. If there was any doubt, he'd not kill the man. The descriptions he'd garnered from the ones he'd killed meant he searched for distinctive marks, body types, and one who was missing an ear.

The man stopped to relieve himself, giving Keithen a clear look. It was one of the men he sought, distinctive because of the long hair that was kept in a plait down his back. The man hesitated as if he sensed he was being watched and looked around.

Keithen moved a foot back and forth, creating a sound like that of an animal foraging.

It was better to do something that would make a person reassured than to stay quiet and invite closer examination. Finally, the man turned away and Keithen emerged from behind a tree, short sword at the ready. Just as he was about to plunge his blade into the man's side, two more men appeared from the hut.

It was a trap.

Chapter Four

Ava stood with her back against the wall. After overhearing plans to trap a man who'd killed several guards, she had to go and ensure it was not the person she suspected. Pausing for a long moment, she listened intently for any sounds of ground patrols. But with all the night noises, it was hard to hear anything past the thudding of her heart.

Bent at the waist, she rushed into the woods and past several huts. Behind one, she crawled under a short shelter and grabbed a bag of clothing. The old woman who lived there had never asked why she kept clothes there. She was probably too scared to ask the laird's daughter and be thrown out.

She lifted a hood to conceal herself and pulled a scarf that she wore around her neck to cover the bottom of her face. Then she bent and pulled a dark cloak over her shoulders and tied it around her neck. The tie would keep the mouth cover and hood in place.

Once she was fully covered from head to toe, she hurried into the forest. Having lived in this place all her life, often spending long days walking and exploring as a child, every area was familiar to her.

Despite the fact the land surrounding the keep was heavily guarded, this portion of the forest rarely was. There was no need, the land leading to it was open, and the only people who lived there were somehow related to the laird.

However, Ava had once caught sight of a man skulking about. He'd not seen her, but she had gotten a clear view of him. When she'd seen Keithen Fraser, it became clear that he was the man she'd spied in the forest. Now, he was to become her betrothed and if he was killing guards, the man would not live long enough to marry her.

She wasn't keen on marriage but was less than enthusiastic for another war between her clan and one that did not deserve it.

It was only moments later that she heard the grunts and clashing of metal, a sure sign of a fight. Slowly, she made her way past low growing brush until she was able to catch sight of who was fighting.

The scene was mesmerizing, three men surrounded one, each one moving with a mixture of care and fury. One would reach forward with a blade, while another would retreat to keep from being cut.

The one in the middle, who was masked, was undoubtedly Keithen Fraser. Not that she could make out much, but his body and the way he moved was very much like the man she'd seen before.

When two men grappled with Keithen, Ava came up behind the third and hit him on the head with a thick branch. The man fell unconscious to the ground just as she hid behind some bushes.

One of the men fighting Keithen stopped and turned to see what had happened but was tripped by the other two fighting. He scrambled away and moved closer to where Ava was hiding. She waited until he came closer and quickly came from behind the tree, swinging the branch and knocking him out as well. She dropped to the ground with him to keep from being seen.

The other two continued to fight until the lone Mackenzie guard realized his comrades were missing.

The man turned in a circle, calling out their names. Before he caught sight of her, she half-crawled to hide behind a different tree. Keithen had backed away, seeming unsure of what had happened. He did not wish to be out in the open. Ava took advantage and hit him, knocking him to the ground.

At this point, noting he was alone, the last guard yelped and said some sort of prayer before turning and running away.

Rumors of the forest being haunted at night during a full moon helped her that night.

"Who are ye?" Keithen asked, pushing to his feet. He swayed just a bit as she backed away.

"Whoever ye are, I will return and finish what I started."

Ava purposely deepened her voice, although she doubted it was deep enough to fool him. "Then ye are a fool."

He didn't reply but, instead, began walking away. Upon nearing the first man on the ground, he lowered and stabbed him in the chest. Then did the same with the second.

Without looking back, he continued walking away.

It had not been a good idea to interfere. But it was better to have done so than to allow the arrogant man to start a war.

Not wishing to be found there if the guard who'd raced away returned with others, Ava dashed away, running as fast as she could through the forest.

Once she arrived at the widow's hut, she quickly removed her disguise and tucked it neatly into the bag.

MOMENTS LATER, SHE slipped in through the kitchen doorway at the keep.

"Ye should not go that way, lass." The cook's head nodded to the doorway. "Yer da and several men are drinking. They've drank quite a bit."

"Thank ye, Maddie," she said to the older woman. "I'll find another way in."

Once Ava was back outside, she hurried down a pathway and to a side door that opened by a staircase.

She hurried up the stairs that were partially hidden from the great room, thanking every saint for her father not seeing her.

Once in her chamber, Ava went to the window and peered out into the night. Her lips curved. It had turned out to be quite an adventure.

"Where is my sister?" Alastair's voice boomed.

Ava quickly kicked off her shoes and pushed them under her bed. She then grabbed a tome from her bedside and leaped onto the bed.

When he opened the door, he found her reading, with part of her hair down and a comb in her opposite hand.

She looked up as if she'd been shocked out of her reading. "What is happening? Is Mother unwell?"

Alastair entered and went to the window where he peered out just like she'd just done. "I was told ye were out."

"When?"

"Now. Someone came to yer chamber and did not see ye." He looked around the room as if sensing her deception. "Men were attacked by a masked assailant."

Ava put the book down and laughed at him. "Do ye think it was me?"

"Of course not." Alastair's expression of annoyance made her want to grin wider.

"Then why are ye coming to seek me?"

"I thought perhaps ye were escaping with whoever it was that attacked our men."

"If I were to escape with someone, it would not be with a man, but with a group of darkly draped women. According to Father, he is to send me away to a nunnery if I do not do as told."

Her brother had never been warm, but he was the closest she had to a friend. "Alastair. Who do ye think ye will marry?"

"Whoever brings our clan something worthwhile." He gave her a one-shouldered shrug. "Personally, I could care less who she is."

"Would ye not like it to be someone ye could grow to care for?"

This time, he looked at her as if she'd gone mad. "Ye have known me all my life. Do ye really think I could grow to care for anyone?"

Her chest constricted, and she fought to swallow. "Does this mean ye could never care for me?"

Although she knew her relatives were hard people, it was unfathomable that they truly had no feelings. Alastair neared and touched the tip of her nose with his index finger. "I will always care for ye, dear sister."

The words rang hollow. It was as if he had to fight to speak kindness. But when she looked up, there was warmth in his gaze.

"I will not run off with a strange man then. I promise."

Alastair looked back out to the night sky. "I will find whoever it is attacking my guards and kill him."

HER HORSE WAS swift, and Ava couldn't hold back laughter when her hair fastenings gave way allowing her tresses to fly around her head. Although the clouds gathered threatening rain, in the moment, she couldn't care less if it stormed.

After managing to slip away unseen, she relished the temporary freedom that would soon be taken from her. She'd not go far, just to the border of her family's lands to the neighboring Chisholm lands. In a small village not too far away, there was a woman who made the most wonderful sweet tarts. Once she purchased a few, she'd eat them all on the ride back.

The only danger riding alone was the proximity to the Fraser land border.

It didn't bother her as she'd gone many times without incident, and as long as she rode fast, the entire trip would not take more than a few hours. That morning, her mother had claimed to feel ill and wished to spend the day in bed. It was common knowledge that the mysterious illnesses were caused by partaking in too many honeyed meads the night before.

Her father and brother were also gone that day to visit her uncle, who'd requested their presence. No doubt, he wished to know the outcome of the alliance between her father and the Fraser.

Ava pushed the thoughts away. What mattered to her was an entire day of freedom to do as she wished.

When she entered the small bakery, no one took notice of the woman dressed in dour clothes wearing a simple kerchief and hunched under a shawl. Finally, when the other customers were gone, she was the only one left. Her mouth watered while watching the woman wrapping the tarts with care.

"Ye should send a messenger to pick them up for ye, Mistress Ava," the woman whispered. "One day, ye will get caught and yer father will not be kind."

Ava shrugged. "He will not find out. Besides, I am to be married and sent away soon. That is why I wish to take extras today. It is doubtful I will be able to get away again." At the words, her bottom lip trembled, and she bit it to keep from looking childish.

"If ye tell me yer wedding day, I will be happy to send tarts," the kind woman said, patting Ava's hand with her own weathered one.

It made her heart leap with joy. "I will send a messenger with coin. Thank ye."

"Nonsense, it will be my gift."

Ava walked out feeling better. She'd missed the occasional escapes for the sweet fruit tarts.

On the ride back, the weather became much cooler, so Ava urged her horse to a faster trot. There were still several hours before she would arrive back at Mackenzie Keep and she wondered if perhaps a thicker cloak would have helped.

In the distance, three horsemen appeared, and she narrowed her eyes in an effort to see them better. Since the village fell under Laird Chisholm's control, the men could be from that clan or hers. There was also the possibility that they were Frasers.

She continued on, thankful she'd plaited her hair and hoped that, from a distance, she would not be recognizable.

Unfortunately, the riders seemed to be in a hurry and soon caught up to her. Just as they rode past, one of them turned to look at her. It was Keithen Fraser.

Her blood went cold, and she shoved the tart she was about to eat back into the sack.

Leaving the other two riders, he rode closer, his green eyes meeting hers. "Why are ye out here, unescorted?"

"I do not have to answer to ye." Ava lifted her chin. "Be on yer way." She made a shooing motion with her hand.

The monster of a beast he rode pawed at the ground. It was either attempting to intimidate her or get her mare's attention. Ava wasn't sure which.

"Why are ye alone?" Keithen looked from her to the direction of her home. "These are dangerous times."

"Aye, I know." She arched an eyebrow, "Some lunatic is killing our guardsmen."

His nostrils flared and eyes narrowed. "Which proves why ye should not be riding alone."

Not wishing to continue the conversation, she urged the mare to continue toward her home. Unfortunately, the stubborn man came alongside her. "I will escort ye halfway. I am sure guards will be out searching for ye."

"They are not."

He gave her an unbelieving glance and then continued looking forward. "Where did ye go?"

Was he attempting a conversation? "I went to the village to get fruit tarts."

"Tarts?"

"Yes."

"Why are women so strong-willed? This is something my sister would do."

"I met yer sister. I liked her."

They rode in silence for a bit, and she considered that being around Keithen was not unpleasant. Nonetheless, the man did not deserve to marry someone who would trick him and could lead him to death. "Ye should not marry me."

It surprised her when he nodded. "I agree."

"But ye are?"

"By my honor, I pledged fealty and obedience to my father and laird. Therefore, I must."

Men and their pledges. Ava wanted to roll her eyes.

"I must thank ye for what ye did for the woman who was brought as a prisoner along with my mother," he said.

It had been horrible to find the poor woman who'd been ravaged and beaten until she was unconscious by the guardsmen. She'd brought several men with her to rescue the woman from their clutches after hearing what they did. Ava had yet to get rid of the images and the many bruises she'd seen when helping to clean the woman's tattered body.

"How does she fare?"

When she looked to him, his face was like stone. "She will never fully recover."

"Ye have feelings for her?" Ava wasn't sure why she asked the question, other than it would matter if they did get married. Better to know if her husband was already involved with another woman.

"Catriona and I grew up together. She is like a sister to me."

Her heart broke for not only the woman, but for Keithen having to witness his lifelong friend so battered and bruised. "I can only offer my regret for what happened…"

"Do not offer something that cannot undo what happened. Yer father ordered her given to those bastards as if she were worthless."

"I had nothing to do with it. Do ye take responsibility for what yer own father does?"

He reached over and yanked on her horse's reins, bringing it to a stop. His eyes bored into hers. "Understand one thing, Ava Mackenzie," he said as his lips twisted in distaste at stating her name. "My father would never commit the atrocities yer father seems to thrive upon."

It was hard to swallow due to the constriction in her throat. There was nothing she could say because, for a long time, she knew everyone either hated or feared her family.

Ava stared at the man that she was to marry and could only see loathing in his eyes. There had to be something she could do to get out of the marriage.

"Release my horse," she uttered. "And be gone from me."

Surprisingly, he did. After turning his horse away, he urged his mount to a gallop.

ONCE SHE NEARED the keep, Ava slowed down and looked over her shoulder, almost expecting to see Keithen following her. The look of disgust and pure hatred he'd given her made Ava shiver with apprehension. Would he be cruel and unjust when they married?

Already, she expected the worst at going to live with Clan Fraser. What was her father thinking sending her to live among people they'd just recently gone to battle with? The Mackenzie warriors had killed many of their people. He was sending her into a lion's den.

Not caring that Lady Fraser was supposedly ill, she stormed into her mother's chamber and pulled back the curtains.

"I must speak to ye," she announced, turning to the bed.

Her mother glowered at her. "Whatever it is that has ye going mad is about to get ye kicked out of my chambers."

Ava ignored her. "Do ye realize Father is sending me to live with people that hate us? Do ye really expect me to live long enough to spy for him? They will no doubt poison my first meal."

Her mother pushed up to a sitting position. "Ye have always been much more like my sister. Much too sensitive. They will do the opposite. They'll make sure ye are protected so as not to earn yer father's ire."

"I saw Keithen Fraser today. I rode to the village on Chisholm lands."

Instead of being upset at her going off without an escort or permission, her mother sighed. "Let me guess, it was a less than friendly exchange."

"Does it not bother ye that I will live with people that hate me?" A tightness in her chest made Ava inhale sharply. "Mother, I am being sent away to a place where I will live in misery."

When her mother patted the bed indicating that she should sit, Ava was apprehensive, but she sat.

"As Mackenzies, we all have a heavy burden to carry. We are strong people who adapt and change in order to protect ourselves. I expect that after ye are there for a spell, ye will learn the best way to live among them."

Something about the sound of her mother's tone gave her pause. Had her mother been different when she arrived at Mackenzie Keep at the age of ten and six? Her mother had grown up in another Clan Mackenzie, from the northern region. Since both the clans were connected, as far as Ava knew, her mother had been immediately accepted. Had her mother always been so cold and distant?

Prompted by the notion, she asked the question that came to mind. "Mother, did ye change upon marrying Father?"

There was a faraway look in her mother's gaze as she directed it toward the window. "Like most young lasses, I wished to live with my family longer. Once I caught yer father's eye, there was nothing that could be done. I was obedient to my father and married."

Her mother's countenance hardened once again. "Ava, ye must be obedient to yer father and then to yer husband. Do yer best, appear to care about those who surround ye. Pleasure yer husband well, so that he will become protective of ye."

Appear to care.

Is that what her mother thought she did? Because in Ava's opinion she'd never once been kind to others, except maybe when her family visited.

Disheartened, she left her mother's chamber and went to her own. There was little to do until last meal and, as usual, her heart felt as heavy as the air inside Mackenzie Keep.

When entering her chamber, she grabbed several items and articles of clothing that were serviceable.

If she was to escape, it had to be that night while her father and brother were gone. Otherwise, another opportunity would be scarce.

CHAPTER FIVE

KEITHEN WOKE WITH a start.

After a long day of patrolling, he'd been exhausted when he went to bed. He'd planned to sleep for a few hours before heading out to the Mackenzie lands. The sunlight through the window told him it was morning and he'd overslept.

Grunting, he turned onto his side and grimaced. The stab wound smarted. He'd have to clean it thoroughly to keep it from festering.

Since it made little sense to go anywhere at that point, he lay on his back and studied the ceiling.

The first image that formed in his mind was Ava Mackenzie's face. The rebellious streak was something he could relate to. Obviously, she escaped for rides and tempted danger as a way of asserting herself. Keithen admired her for it. However, it went no further. She was a Mackenzie, which meant her father's blood ran through her veins.

Admittedly, there had been a hint of vulnerability about her, and perhaps she could be kind. After all, if it were not for Ava, Catriona could have been killed.

At thinking of Catriona, his chest constricted. Would his poor friend ever recover? Probably not. There was hope that, with time, she would grow stronger and get past the horrible experience, at least a bit.

At the sound of knocks, he called out for whoever it was to enter. It was Broden. "I've not known ye to sleep in."

Keithen sat up and pretended annoyance, although he was glad his friend had come and dragged him away from thoughts of Ava Makenzie. "Since when do ye visit bedchambers? Do ye wish to embroider next?"

"I prefer to weave," Broden replied in a dry tone and went to peer out the window. "The contingent of Ross guards have arrived."

"How many?'

"Fifty as agreed, no more, no less."

It was admirable that the Ross kept his word. They'd been promised fifty men who would come and live there. Some would rotate back and forth to Ross lands, but most had volunteered to remain.

"Who leads them?"

"Ewan Ross," Broden replied. "I do not care for him."

Although Keithen recalled the amicable man, he wasn't sure what about him would make him unlikeable. "What did he do?"

Broden's face went hard. "He annoys me."

A chuckle escaped from Keithen. He slid from the bed and dressed. "Is my father up?"

"Not as yet."

MOMENTS LATER, THEY exited out to the busy courtyard. Horses were being led away by stable lads, while more lads rushed forward to get other steeds. The warriors who arrived milled about, sacks of belongings at their feet as they studied the surroundings.

A good fighter always familiarized himself with exits, vulnerable locations, and how many people were about.

Keithen knew that Ross Keep was much larger than his, which meant the Ross guards were probably used to nice accommodations.

Upon learning the number of new arrivals to come, his father had ordered that new structures be built that would rival any at larger homes. Each warrior would have a private space, comfortable bedding and a window.

A well was dug and set up in the center of two U-shaped compounds, along with tables, chairs and a firepit.

A part of him was excited to show them their accommodations, which they'd share with twenty Fraser guards.

Most of the Fraser guards lived either in the village or on farms when not on duty, which left only twenty to live in the keep. The Fraser men had been more than willing to move into the newer accommodations and were already settled.

Ewan Ross came forward, the familiar Ross hazel gaze meeting his directly. "We arrived a bit earlier than planned. The horses were anxious for the travel." The corners of his lips lifted while he was speaking, giving the illusion of a friendly demeanor. Although the man was easy to get along with, Keithen had seen him in battle. Ewan Ross was not only deadly accurate with the bow and arrow, but a force when fighting hand-to-hand.

"Welcome," Keithen replied, gripping the man's hand. "We are grateful for yer laird's support."

Broden stood just to the side, his gaze flat. "Once the laird greets yer men, they will be fed."

As if conjured, several men and women appeared with long wooden planks and began setting up tables just outside the kitchen. Lads rushed past with benches they'd pulled from beside the stables, all which had been built for the new larger guard.

With precision, everything was set up under the watchful eye of Eileen, the head cook. Moments later, six long tables had been placed where they would permanently remain. A covering would be added soon to provide protection during the colder months. The carpenters would probably be sent for later that day.

"Have yer men line up. I will inform my father of yer arrival," Keithen told Ewan and walked to the front entrance.

Ewan Ross and whoever the other head guard was would be offered rooms inside. This meant he had to ensure to remind his mother the chambers needed to be prepared just off the servant quarters where Broden also had a room.

"There ye are," his father said, appearing at the top of the stairs. "I wondered if ye were outside yet."

"I came to seek ye," Keithen said, stopping his father's progress. "Father, we must discuss the future with the council. With a force like the Ross behind us, we should not have to join in marriage with the Mackenzie. Laird Ross may pull back his support if he learns of our intentions of an alliance with the bastard Mackenzie."

Lines of weariness were apparent on Laird Fraser's brow and tight lines formed around his mouth. "We will have to speak to the Ross prior to him receiving the news from elsewhere. I am not sure there is a way to avoid what has been set in motion."

"There has to be a way…"

His father placed a hand on his shoulder. "Believe me when I say I understand how ye feel. I don't wish to have an alliance with the Mackenzie any more than with the devil himself. But we must consider the fate of our people. Fifty new warriors seems like a great number, but not when we compare it the five hundred the Mackenzie can send to attack us if we cross him."

Together, they went outside. Keithen at his father's side, they welcomed and thanked the men for being there to support their people.

Keithen's heart broke, knowing it was not easy for his father to admit they needed the support of another clan to keep their own people safe.

The new arrivals were then shown their accommodations. It made Keithen proud to see the expressions of surprise and admiration from the newcomers. Each man chose a room and placed their belongings inside. Once they were settled, they would be fed and then allowed to rest for the day.

The following day, assignments would be given. Training

would begin so that the newly arrived force would become accustomed to and familiar with the Fraser guard.

Ewan and another lead guard were to be given rooms in the keep that were larger than the ones at the guard houses.

Moments later, Ewan joined Keithen, Broden and Laird Fraser in the great room. Ewan silently waited to be spoken to by the laird. Laird Fraser motioned for the men to sit and servants brought them a morning meal.

Already, villagers had begun arriving for whatever business they were to seek council from his father for, while at the same time hoping to be fed.

The cooks would be busy that morning, it seemed. Women had already been sent for from the village and, thankfully, there was plenty of food left from the night before to help serve the guards.

"I pray yer cousin, Laird Ross, fares well," Laird Fraser said to Ewan.

Ewan nodded. "Quite well, aye. His second child was recently born. Another son, to be named Lachlan Alexander."

"That is indeed good news," Laird Fraser said.

Ewan produced several envelopes. "From yer daughter."

Laird Fraser's lips curved. "She certainly enjoys writing. Yer messengers must be glad for the reprieve of ye bringing these."

The men chuckled at the truth of it. Keithen's sister, Esme, was newly married to a Ross. She'd moved to live there, but either visited frequently or sent letters. They expected that once Esme became a mother, perhaps she would not travel as much. But none of them were willing to wager on it.

When a servant neared, his father gave her the letters. "Give these to my wife promptly."

"Yes, Laird," the woman replied and hurried away.

If there was a message from Laird Ross, it would be delivered in the privacy of his father's study. Since Ewan showed no hurry, it was obvious there was either no message or one that was only a cursory greeting.

AFTER THE MEAL, Keithen and the men, along with council, were to meet in his father's study. But his father stopped him, taking his forearm. "See about the concerns of the people. What we have to discuss with the council is not as important."

"If it has to do with my marriage and the handling of the new guards, it is very much important to me."

When his father's right eyebrow lifted, he turned on his heel and went to the high board.

Upon sitting, a farmer rushed forward, hauling with him a crying young woman. They were followed by a young man he recognized. The young man often delivered oats and whey for the animals from his father's farm.

He studied the people before him, from the angry father, to the crying woman, to the young man who looked to be more annoyed than anything.

Curious, he motioned to the father. "Why have ye brought yer daughter here?"

"She insists on marrying this…this boy. I will not allow it. I offer her instead to come work here in yer father's service."

Leaning forward, Keithen studied the father. "What problem do ye have with Tavish?"

At mentioning the boy by name, the farmer frowned. "He is not good enough."

The young woman looked over her shoulder to Tavish. "We love each other. That is all that matters, is it not, Laird Keithen?"

Keithen studied Tavish for a moment. The young man had yet to step forward. "Tell her the truth." It was obvious Tavish had no desire to marry the girl but was too kind to speak it.

"I do not wish to marry as yet," Tavish said, looking straight at the young woman who once again began to cry and raced from the room.

"Why would ye say that?" the father demanded.

"See about yer daughter," Keithen said, sending the man away. Tavish gave him a grateful nod and followed them out.

As annoying as most of the requests and concerns were, with

each person he dealt with, the sense of responsibility for the people grew. Keithen studied their faces, acknowledging how much the people depended on his family to care, lead and protect them.

There were only a few people left milling about when a guard came in from the courtyard and motioned for him to come out.

"There are four men here to speak to ye. They wear no markings of clan affiliation and have asked specifically for ye."

Keithen walked out and hurried to the gates where four mounted men waited, just outside.

Upon seeing him, one dismounted and neared. He kept his voice low. "I am Gavin Mackenzie. I came to ask ye if my cousin, Ava Mackenzie, is here."

For some reason, his stomach tightened at the words. "No. She is not. Why do ye come to seek me about it?"

The man looked over his shoulder to ensure they were not heard. "Ava is missing, and my aunt does not wish the Mackenzie to know. She must have slipped out sometime during the night."

"How is that possible? Yer keep is heavily fortified."

The man shrugged. "Ava is quite…proficient at finding ways to do so."

"I will do a discrete search of the surrounding areas. If I find her, I will ensure to escort her home."

The warrior met his gaze. "We were told she and ye met and spoke. Did she say something that may help us find her?"

Keithen considered their conversation for a moment. "She rides to the village on Chisholm lands to purchase tarts. Perhaps that is a place to look. Ava seemed very familiar with the roads there and back."

When the men rode off, Keithen remained standing for a long while, considering what to do next.

He went to the guard who'd come for him. "The man remembers me from an archery competition. He seems intent on competing again."

The guard grinned. "No doubt, he has been practicing since

ye beat him."

"Aye," Keithen replied and headed back inside. The sooner he took care of what the people needed, the faster he could go and try to help find Ava. Not to mention, there was still the matter of revenge. Three men remained. If only he'd not been thwarted by the masked idiot, there would be only two. The two men he killed that night were not the men he was searching for.

Then again, there was the possibility he'd be dead.

CHAPTER SIX

THE WIND MANAGED to make it through the gaps in the walls of the small abandoned cottage. When it had begun to rain, Ava had managed to find shelter there the night before.

Shivering, Ava pulled her cloak tightly around herself and wondered what to do next. She'd ridden south for several hours until she'd become lost.

Deciding to wait until sunrise to get her bearings, she was annoyed when the day was much too cloudy and dreary, making it impossible to figure out where the sun was. It would not do to remain somewhere that could be on enemy lands. She got up from the small cot and stalked out.

After gathering some kindling and a few branches, she returned inside and started a fire in the tiny hearth. The cottage must have belonged to a family displaced by her father, as many of their wares remained.

It was sad that his lust for power affected so many, Ava considered as she picked up a broom and began sweeping away months of dirt and dust. Moving about and doing something always helped her think.

An hour later, the tiny space was cleaner and warmer. She boiled water in a pot over the fire and added a few of her horse's oats, which she'd share with him until she was able to purchase food somewhere along her travels.

The plan was to go to a large village where no one knew her. Pretending to be a poor widow, she could join a community. Although she had no trade, she was an efficient weaver and could make nice blankets and shawls.

With the coin she'd brought with her, it would be more than enough to establish herself somewhere and never have to be a Mackenzie again.

It was much later that day when Ava went out to check on her steed. The animal seemed content enough under the small shelter attached to the cottage. After fetching water and feeding him, she walked around in an effort to familiarize herself with the surroundings. Rather than head in a direction she was not sure of, Ava decided to remain there. She'd have to spend another night, so it was best to know if anyone lived nearby.

After walking just a few minutes, the sounds of horses caught her attention and she fell to the ground to keep from being seen.

A group of eight men on horseback patrolled. They wore clan colors and were obviously guardsmen. Ava immediately recognized the tartan and she blew out a breath. She'd gone in the wrong direction because the men were definitely Frasers.

It was not the best situation to be on Fraser lands. If she were found alone, the men would not hesitate to assault her.

Heart thundering, she remained flat on the ground, praying they did not notice any smoke coming from the cottage.

Her worst fears materialized when one of the men stopped and looked around. He seemed to sense something was amiss. Head down, Ava remained frozen in place, unable to breathe.

Just then, a horseman appeared and neared the guardsmen. She didn't dare lift her head to see who it was. Instead, she listened intently.

Moments later, all the men rode away. Ava couldn't believe her luck. Ever so slowly, she crept backward then stood and hurried to the cottage.

Once inside, she doused what was left of the fire and lowered to a chair. It was imperative to figure out where she was. With a twig, she began drawing a map from memory. There was no sound of water outside, therefore she'd missed the river's edge. Instead of going directly south to MacBean lands as had been her plan, she'd diverted southwest and straight into Fraser territory.

She would have to take a chance and go back outside to try to gauge where, exactly, she was. There was no other way to figure it out. Thankfully, the clouds had begun to dissipate and, soon, she'd be able to track the sun's descent.

Letting out a sigh, she stood and went to the window and peered out. There didn't seem to be anyone about. As much as she wanted to go outside, terror kept her from reaching for the door. There wasn't any choice, she could not remain there. Sooner rather than later, she'd be found out and the consequences could prove horrific.

The horse made a sound and Ava wondered if someone was out there. She hurried to the back of the cottage and leaned on the wall, hoping to hear better. But the animal settled and was silent.

Everything was going wrong. It was as if fate wanted her to be in a horrible situation, married to someone who detested her and her family, albeit with good reason.

Knowing there was no choice but to go out and scout, Ava hurried to the door. After a sharp breath, she opened it to find that a man blocked her way out.

Ava shrieked and stumbled backward. She would have fallen if not for the strong hands gripping hers and pulling her upright.

"Yer family is looking for ye," Keithen said matter-of-factly, looking around her in case someone else was there. "Why are ye here?"

Not quite recovered from the scare, all she did was look at him, her eyes wide. If he decided to kill her, which she believed he was capable of, no one would ever be the wiser.

Keithen took her elbow and guided her to a chair. "Sit."

Instead of sitting, Ava hurried around the table to put space between them. He was larger, stronger and even faster, but she would fight until the bitter end. Narrowing her eyes, she watched him closely for any movement.

For a moment, they locked gazes. His expression was unclear, his thoughts a mystery. Even though she hoped hers were as well, Ava knew better. The terror she felt at the moment, the knowledge it was possibly her last day was impossible to keep hidden.

"We must figure out a way to get ye back home before yer father uses the absence as an excuse to attack us again," Keithen said, pulling back a chair, turning it and then straddling the spindly piece. "Yer cousin," he tapped the side of his head attempting to remember the name, "Gavin, I believe, came to see me. It seems yer mother is keeping yer absence hidden."

"Why would ye help me? This is the perfect opportunity…" Ava stopped speaking, realizing she was an idiot.

Keithen's eyes narrowed. "Is that what ye hoped? To be killed? Is the reason ye came to my family's lands an attempt to die?"

"No. Of course not. There was no moon visible and I became disoriented. I planned to head to MacBean lands and then further south."

"I see." His jaw flexed. "I am not sure if ye disappearing would help or hinder my clan."

Ava grasped on the opportunity. "Help me escape. My father will not be able to force yer clan to any agreement if I am gone."

He seemed to consider it for a moment. "I must think on it."

"There is no time," Ava said, moving closer now that she felt better about her chances of living. "Did ye plan to kill me?"

"I did not." The man frowned. "I do not kill defenseless women. Although, I have a hard time thinking of ye as defenseless."

He eyed the visible short sword at her waist and the corners of his lips lifted. For an inexplicable reason, for the first time in her life, Ava felt as if she could make a friend. It was the most ridiculous notion, but something about Keithen Fraser gave her ease and, even stranger, comfort.

"Very well, I will help ye," he finally said. "But first, I must go to my home and create some sort of reason for my absence."

"It should only take a day, two at the most," Ava said, "I am a good rider."

"Aye, I have seen," he replied. "I will return in the morning. Meanwhile…" he looked around. "Have ye eaten anything?"

"Oats."

"Come." He held out his hand. "Tis a better way to hide ye."

Unsure why she did so, Ava took his hand and, together, they went outside. A short time later, with a hood over her head, they arrived at his home.

Ava had never seen anything like it. Guards and people mingled about, chatting, laughing and sitting at long tables, sharing a meal. Everyone seemed at ease, even the warriors who eyed her with curiosity.

Upon dismounting, she hurried after Keithen into the main house where the same kind of atmosphere took place in the great room. No one took much notice of them as they made their way up a set of stairs and down a corridor.

"Early for a tryst," a guard said with a chuckle.

"It's never too early," Keithen replied and laughed.

With a firm hold on her elbow, he pulled her into a bedchamber and closed the door behind them.

Ava removed her hood and glared up at him. "Ye would allow them to think I am some sort of whore for hire?"

"Tis best to hide in plain view at times," Keithen replied with a one-shoulder shrug that made her huff out loud. "They do not suspect it is ye. That is for sure." Then holding out a hand, he motioned around the room. "Make yerself comfortable. I will get ye some food. Do not open the door or speak to anyone. Am I understood?"

When he left, she took her cloak off and wandered around in

a circle, much too restless to sit. This had to be the worst escape ever. Somehow, she'd ended up hiding in the exact place she was fighting to avoid.

Sounds from outside caught her attention and she hurried to the window. Was it possible her father was there to attack already?

Instead, she was greeted by the most interesting sight. Men were erecting tents outside the walls. Hammering and sawing began in earnest, while others set up what would be a huge bonfire.

Several carts traveled toward the keep from the direction of a village and the guardsmen atop the gates waved down to those beneath, seeming to call out greetings.

A horrific thought came to mind. Was the bonfire for her? Was she to be burned at the stake as entertainment for the people who were gathering?

What better way to repay her father for what her clan had done. It could be that the men who'd ridden by the cottage earlier had, indeed, seen her and set all of this in motion. Keithen had then been sent to lure her here.

Her hands shook. She was inside the keep and probably locked in the chamber. After grabbing her cloak, she took measured steps to the doorway. Even if she could open the door, of course there would be a guard outside in the corridor.

When her fingers grasped the door handle and it opened freely, she let out a long breath. Ever so slowly, she opened the door and peered out.

The corridor was devoid of anyone. Strange. Perhaps it was part of the game. She was prey after all.

"And who might ye be?"

Ava whirled around, finding herself face to face with Lady Fraser, whose eyes looked like they were about to pop from her head.

"Oh, goodness," both said at the same time.

Just then, a chambermaid and a guard came around the corner. Both stopped in their tracks. The guard pulled a sword and pointed it at Ava.

Ava drew hers and took a defensive stance.

The chambermaid screamed, which caused more guards and other people, including the laird, to come running.

AVA HAD NEVER seen so much pacing in her life. Obviously, it was a Fraser trait. Laird Fraser paced up and down the side of the room, while Keithen paced across the center. Lady Fraser sat next to Ava with her hands clutched in her lap.

They'd moved to the sitting room, where they'd waited for Keithen, who'd returned from the kitchen with a tray of food to find that she was no longer in his bedchamber.

"Of course, ye must marry immediately," Lady Fraser said to no one in particular. "Ye were found in my son's bedchamber. News will get to yer father eventually."

Too hungry to think, Ava reached for another slice of thinly cut meat and buttered bread. While eating, she studied the dynamics in the room. Just then, an older man entered and stopped short at seeing her and looked to the laird.

"Is this her?" He looked to Ava. "I am the village vicar. Are ye Miss Ava Mackenzie?" His gaze moved from her to the laird. "Is this lady here of her own will?"

"Sit down, Jonah. We must think," Lady Fraser snapped. "Of course, she is not here by force. She was brought here to hide by my foolish son."

The vicar glared at Keithen who blew out a breath and glared at Ava.

"They must marry immediately," the vicar pronounced. "Immediately," he reiterated.

"I agree," Lady Fraser said.

The laird neared and met Ava's gaze. "I am afraid it is the

only way to keep yer father from accusing us of kidnapping ye."

"I can explain to him…" Ava started, but stopped speaking at realizing her father would never believe a word she said.

"Are we to be star-crossed secret lovers who snuck away to marry?" Keithen's tone dripped with sarcasm. "I am sure he will not be pleased whether we marry in secret or not."

"Nonetheless, my mind has been made up." Laird Fraser motioned to the vicar. "Now, if ye will."

The vicar cleared his throat, his pleasant face softening as he looked to Ava. "Ye should not have run away with a man if ye did not wish to marry."

Her back teeth ached from biting down so hard. "Perhaps he should not have dragged me away if he did not wish to marry."

Everyone turned to Keithen who returned a bored look. "If it must be done, let us get on with it. Her disappearance cannot be kept secret for much longer."

Just then, shouts sounded and everyone hurried to the window.

"With all this, I'd forgotten about the harvest festival," Lady Fraser said. "We cannot very well send everyone away."

"It can be a wedding celebration," the ever-clueless vicar suggested.

Laird Fraser sighed. "I do not believe Laird Mackenzie will appreciate his lack of an invitation."

"There is that," the vicar acceded.

Moments later, Ava and Keithen stood in front of several gathered people as they were married by a jovial vicar. The entire time, Ava wanted to scream in frustration. How was it that she was about to end up doing the exact thing she'd tried to run away from?

Keithen's flat gaze met hers as he said his vows. Nothing about the way he pronounced each word seemed sincere. Not that she would ever claim to know him well, but from the tone in which he spoke and the slight furrow between his brows, he did not mean the words.

The laird and several council members exchanged looks that gave her chills. Something was afoot. They planned to somehow use this marriage against her father.

Once the vows were exchanged, Ava was immediately guided back to Keithen's room.

The vicar, his mother and two others whom she refused to look upon entered the room to witness the joining. Of course, it was necessary so that neither party could later attempt to end the marriage by citing there was no consummation.

The entire process was mechanical. She'd barely been pushed back onto the bed before Keithen entered her, pushing in once, twice and then one last time before pulling out.

Humiliated, she slid up to sit as the people filed from the room. This was the second time it had happened. The first time had been much more painful as she'd been a terrified virgin. This time, however, she would describe it as much more hurtful.

Keithen went to stand by the window. "We will travel to yer keep in the morning."

"Are ye not sending a messenger instead?"

"A messenger has already been dispatched."

Ava studied her husband with new insight.

Standing at the window, with the physique of a well-trained warrior, Keithen had thick muscled arms, powerful legs and wide shoulders. His hair fell just past his ears in silky brown waves that contradicted every other part of him. He was handsome and hard, but she'd noticed how his face softened when speaking to his mother.

And yet, she knew whatever would happen the next day would forever change the course of her life. "Why are we returning to my home tomorrow?"

"To return ye to yer family."

TO REJECT AND return a woman to her family was one of the most humiliating things that could be done to a laird's daughter. Not only would the Mackenzie have to accept her back, but he would be powerless to do anything in retaliation.

Even the Mackenzie could not get away from the insult.

Ava would not be able to show herself in public for a long time. Although most would suspect the cause of rejection was the fact Clan Fraser and Clan Mackenzie were enemies, the gossips would enjoy inventing reasons for it.

Keithen had ensured he did not spend his seed into his new wife so that there would be no possible way for her to become with child.

The entire consummation had felt wrong. As he paced in the chamber while she slept, he could not shake the heavy weight of guilt.

It was unfair to Ava. She'd done nothing to deserve such treatment, but it was inevitable. Everything had been set in motion. The next day, he, along with a contingent of warriors, would escort Ava back to Mackenzie Keep. Once there, she would ride alone to the entrance and he would never see her again.

EVEN MORE PEOPLE had gathered for the harvest festival. In an effort to keep Ava's departure quiet for a long as possible, the party was forced to leave through a back gate.

Keithen rode beside Ava as they made their way through the forest that would eventually lead them into Mackenzie lands. He'd purposely chosen a route that would keep them from being too visible.

They'd been traveling for a couple of hours when he slid a look to Ava. She rode with pride, her back straight and her eyes staring straight ahead.

"Do ye need to stop?"

She shook her head. "No."

Keithen had the feeling that if he pushed her to speak, she would crumble and lose the hold she stubbornly kept on her emotions.

The strength she showed was extraordinary. The woman would be his wife for life and yet, at the same time, he would not have any type of relationship with her. Now he wondered many things about her, making him wish they'd perhaps gotten an opportunity to speak more.

"Stop staring at me," she snapped.

"I am sorry that this has to happen." Keithen searched for words to try to explain, but it was ridiculous. What was happening could not be softened by words.

It was late in the day when they finally caught sight of Mackenzie Keep. They'd ridden all day and had not stopped, Ava refusing to do so.

When they neared, everyone stopped except for Ava.

Just outside the walls of Mackenzie Keep, lines of horsemen flanked the gates, two people, also on horseback, remained in front of the rest.

Back straight, his wife rode without hesitating until she disappeared as the gates closed behind her.

KEITHEN ENTERED HIS father's study the next morning. Unable to sleep, he'd been up half the night, wondering how bad Ava's return had been for his wife. No doubt, the insult of her being returned was something the Mackenzie would take great offense to and he would be slow to forgive them for it. He probably never would forgive them.

"A messenger arrived first thing this morning," Laird Fraser said, waving him to come closer.

Taking a deep breath, he met his father's gaze. "What is the message?"

"Assurance that the insult to his daughter is not taken lightly. He pledges to ensure ye pay for it. Additionally, he proclaims that although we are united because of the marriage, he holds us in low regard."

"Low regard? I expected worse," Keithen replied.

"His actual words are 'lower than swine'."

"Ah."

"It had to be done. We could not risk having her here."

As much as he agreed with his father, a part of him still hated how, through no fault of her own, Ava was used as a pawn by both her father and her husband.

Chapter Seven

One year later

"That ye continue on this quest is madness," Catriona said, her brown eyes boring into his.

Keithen took a bite of an apple and studied his friend as she walked about the garden collecting flowers. As the months had passed, she'd become much stronger. Although she was still overly cautious and rarely smiled, a bit of the old Catriona had begun to emerge.

"It is not done yet," he said, referring to the fact he continued to hunt the guards responsible for her attack. In truth, he'd not wished to speak of it. It was best not to remind her of the past, but it was Catriona who'd brought the subject up.

"I wish to put that behind me, and I cannot if I have to worry about ye." Catriona lifted the basket she'd been placing the clipped blooms into and motioned to the house with her head. "Tis almost midday. I will go see if yer mother requires help with preparations for Esme's visit."

His sister, along with several from Clan Ross, were due to arrive in the following days, which meant he'd be forced to remain home.

"I must go to the village. Let Mother know I will not return for last meal." Heading to the stables, he hoped to find the information he'd been waiting on.

KEITHEN WALKED INTO the dim tavern that was located in the same tiny village on Chisholm land that he'd once caught Ava returning from. He immediately recognized who he was there to see. A lone man sat at a back table with a tankard at his elbow.

Keithen neared and sat at a different table but faced the man who met his eyes for a moment.

"Ale," he told the woman who shuffled over and she hurried away to fetch his beverage.

"There will be a peculiar thing in the eastern forest the next two nights," the man said, looking in his direction. "A lone sheep is easy to hunt."

He nodded and studied the worn wood of the tabletop. "I will hunt."

"Be with care, sheep can bite," came the cryptic reply.

He wondered what the man meant by the last words, but he could not ask as the stranger walked past, grabbed the bag of coins Keithen had set on the table and then slipped out.

Once he drank the ale, Keithen went to his horse and considered the best route to go to the forest on Mackenzie lands in order to avoid detection. Of the areas around Mackenzie Keep, the eastern territory was the most dangerous. Guards constantly patrolled that portion because it bordered several other clans, Clan Ross included.

Although his clan was allied with the Ross, it didn't mean he wouldn't be questioned if caught by them as well. There was much to worry about and plan for.

However, if he managed to kill one of the bastards who'd attacked Catriona, it would be well worth it. He knew exactly who he was hunting that day. It was the man with a reddish birthmark on the right side of his face.

He'd failed to protect her before, had allowed not only

Catriona, but his own mother to fall into the hands of abusive men. So now it was his responsibility to ensure it never happened again.

There would be no rest for him until every man who had dared to touch Catriona or his mother was dead. He'd managed to kill three, and each kill had been satisfactory.

Just then, a familiar horseman appeared. Ewan Ross dismounted and sauntered over to him. "I thought ye'd be in this area."

"What are ye doing here?" Keithen could not believe his bad luck. Not only did he have little time to get to where he was going, but now had to figure out a way to get rid of Ewan.

"Looking for ye," Ewan replied, his keen gaze moving from him to the horse. "Ruari asked that I keep an eye on ye. He told me what ye are doing."

Keithen had wondered why it had been almost impossible to get away in the last few months. He'd managed to get away from his keep once. But other than that, each time he'd set up a meeting with the man who'd just left the tavern, something had gone awry.

"It's been ye that have impeded my progress then?" Keithen asked with a glare. "Do ye realize how much it has cost?"

"Yer life perhaps."

"Return to the keep. Stay out of this. It has nothing to do with ye or my sister's husband."

Ewan shrugged. "Matters naught to me. However, think of Catriona and what this would do to her. If ye get yerself killed, it would only add to her burden."

Disgruntled, but with no other choice, Keithen rode back to his keep. There wasn't much to be done with Ewan Ross following him.

As night fell, he considered that he'd not have another opportunity for a long time yet.

KEITHEN, EWAN AND several guards rode out as part of their daily patrol the next morning. Keithen studied the Ross archer. "Ye did not grow up with Malcolm and his brothers, did ye?" he asked, referring to Laird Ross.

"I grew up on Uist." Ewan looked in the direction of his home with a faraway look. "I have always lived by the sea."

Although he'd never been to Uist, Keithen had traveled to the shore several times. He studied the man. "Why did ye leave?"

"Riders approaching," Ewan said. In the distance, a group of men on horseback galloped toward them.

The Fraser tartan was instantly recognizable and Keithen relaxed. Upon seeing Keithen, the man in the lead signaled for the group to slow and they came to a stop.

"What is going on?" Keithen asked.

"Mackenzie warriors are out in force, searching out a band of men. They are on attack."

As a group, they rode hard until reaching Fraser Keep. Keithen called out for the gates to be closed and ordered every guard to his post.

His father, upon being informed of the possible threat, sent a group of warriors to protect the village.

Keithen stalked from one side of the roof to the other, his gaze on the surrounding land. "Where are the scouts?"

"It will take time to find out what happened," his father said. But he, too, kept watch toward the north.

It was hours later that a group of Mackenzie warriors appeared. They rode fast until they arrived at the gates.

Along with the laird, Keithen hurried to the courtyard. "I will speak to them," Keithen said, placing an arm protectively in front of his father. "Ye remain here."

His father remained silent as the gates were opened and four of the twenty or so entered. One man dismounted and walked toward Keithen and his father, his path blocked by Fraser guards, swords drawn.

After a flat look around, the man met first his father's then Keithen's eyes. "We search for a group of men who may have come here for refuge."

"No one has come here as of late," his father replied in a strong voice.

The man met his father's gaze for a long moment as if attempting to sense if he spoke the truth. "They have much to answer for."

Keithen's chest tightened. "Is my wife safe?"

The man's upper lip curled in distaste. "What would it matter to ye?"

In truth, he had no claim when it came to Ava. After all, he'd rejected her and turned his back on the woman. Yet it did matter to him. He didn't wish anything bad to happen to her.

"If men come seeking refuge, I am not sure I could turn them away without knowing what they are being charged with," his father told them.

The visitor looked over his shoulder to the other three. Whatever happened, it was quite dire, it seemed. "I can only say that there was an unprovoked occurrence to our clan. We will eventually find them, and they will be punished."

As dictated by Highland custom, the men were fed and offered rest for a night. They accepted the food but turned down the offer to remain and were soon on their way.

"IT IS FRUITLESS to try to figure out what happened." Keithen's Uncle Hamish and Aunt Matilde, who lived just a few miles away, arrived upon hearing about the Mackenzie warriors coming to their land.

His father sat back, absently rolling a glass of whisky between his hands.

"The scout has returned," a guard announced from the door and they all reacted by getting to their feet.

The man who entered had been in his father's service for as long as Keithen could remember. First as a stable lad, and later, much too small in size for battle, as an archer. A fast rider and quite sly, he now served as a scout.

"What news do ye bring, John?" his father asked impatiently.

John's face lit up. "The Mackenzie is either dead or dying. Apparently, while returning from a visit to his brother with a small escort, he was shot several times with arrows. Whoever it was remained so well hidden that the laird's guards could not find him. Torn with having to save his life or try to find the attacker, they chose to take him to the keep before dispatching warriors to hunt those responsible."

"When did this happen?" Keithen asked, feeling relieved that it was not Ava who had been injured in some way. Although, he supposed, she would be saddened at losing her father.

"At dawn, today," the scout said.

They settled into their chairs, each quietly considering the ramifications of what would happen if Laird Mackenzie died.

"His son, Alastair, is not much better than his father," Keithen's uncle said. "Perhaps not as ruthless. I am not sure."

Broden, who was also in the room, grunted. "I competed against him during the games a year ago. He was actually somewhat pleasant."

"Taking over as laird could bring out the worst or the best in a man," Laird Fraser replied. "I wonder what this means for us. I cannot see how it will impact us in any way."

For a long time, the men sat around the table deep in thought, every so often saying something that occurred to them. The truth of it was, they would eventually find out if the Mackenzie lived or died.

Keithen walked out of his father's study and out to the courtyard. There was work to be done. The duties of everyday life called.

However, his thoughts kept returning to Ava.

How was his wife faring?

CHAPTER EIGHT

"MOTHER!" AVA CALLED out, pounding on the closed door. "Open the door."

After a long moment, the heavy door was opened, and she entered her parents' bedchamber and had to swallow to keep from gagging. The mercurial stench of blood and vomit was thick in the air, mixing with the pungent smell of whatever herbs the healer used.

There were several others in the room, but only the healer and his helpers surrounded the bed where her father lay.

Lady Mackenzie sat by the window, a handkerchief over her mouth and Alastair looked on from the corner.

Ava neared the bed and peered down at her father. If not for the fact that the healer continued cleaning a seeping wound, she would have thought him to be already dead. His skin and lips blended in an alarmingly pale shade of gray. His closed eyes were sunken.

Instead of the intimidating persona her father ensured to always maintain, he looked to have shrunk and disappeared into the bedding. Exposed from the waist up, she could see where the arrows had pierced the flesh, the wounds concentrated in the center of his chest. Three punctures in all.

"Did ye get all the arrows out cleanly?" Ava asked the healer who frowned at her but nodded.

After touching his forehead and noting that he was not feverish, Ava then placed two fingers at his neck. Her father's pulse was so weak she could barely feel it.

There was little doubt in her mind that he was dying, but she kept the fact to herself. A strange sense of calm came over her and she wondered if it was good or bad. Whether her father lived or died should be upsetting and yet the sense in the room was more one of acceptance.

From where she sat, her mother leaned forward to see what Ava was doing. Ava touched one of the puncture wounds, testing it.

"Come away from the bed," her mother said in a dry tone. "Allow the healer to do what he has to do to save yer father."

Ava met the healer's gaze. "There is nothing further to be done. Ye should allow him to rest."

The healer's shoulders fell in obvious relief. He would not be blamed for the laird's death if he followed the man's own daughter's advice.

With little to do when she was young, Ava had spent weeks in the tutelage of her grandmother, who was a celebrated healer. It was said no healer could ever compare to the woman, who healed many from their deathbeds.

Although she rarely was called on to heal lately because her father had no trust in her abilities, she regularly met with the official healer to discuss the best ways to care for the ill and injured.

The healer nodded. "Bring fresh water and clean sheets," he instructed.

Together with the healer, Ava helped wash her father and wrap him in clean bandages. He was then laid atop fresh linens.

The windows were opened to allow fresh air in, which her mother tried to argue against.

"Ye cannot allow it. The air will cause him harm," she told

the healer.

The healer led Lady Mackenzie to the bed. "Tis best ye say yer farewell. I am afraid there is little that can be done for yer husband now."

⋙⋘

AVA LISTENED IN when the Mackenzie council met. Everyone, including her brother, was much too preoccupied to tell her to leave the room.

The fall of Clan Mackenzie, the most feared group of warriors was swift. As soon as news spread of the laird's death, it was as if a dam broke and, immediately, allies broke ties with them. There was little to do as they could not fight battles on every side.

Alastair did what he could to keep some of the smaller alliances but, for the most part, no one wanted anything to do with him.

It became evident that there had been clandestine meetings between lairds. They'd been waiting for something like this to happen in order to end the alliances and form their own.

Now with Clans Matheson, Macrae, Chisholm and Urquhart joining with a portion of the southern McLeods and MacDonnells, they became much too great a force for the Mackenzies to overtake.

Therefore, within weeks of Laird Mackenzie's passing, Alastair inherited a much smaller, and weaker clan.

Ava entered the great room one afternoon to find her brother and one of their uncles, who'd become Alastair's advisor, sitting at a table. She neared and waited for Alastair to take notice.

"Ye called for me?" Ava asked.

Alastair looked to her for a moment. "Aye, ye must go with our uncle to speak to the Fraser."

Her stomach sunk. "Ye cannot expect me to face them. Not after what they did."

"We are allied with them and must ensure it remains that way. Without them, our southern borders are vulnerable."

"What ye fear are the repercussions of what our clan did to many for years. Killing, stealing and overtaking people just for gain of power. Why would the Frasers want to help us? Our clan attacked them and then forced them to accept a marriage that brought nothing but shame to us."

Her brother jumped to his feet. "Enough! Stop speaking. Ye will do as ye are told."

"I cannot. It would be as if I am a dog begging for a scrap."

The slap across her face was so hard it sent her backward several steps, but Ava was much too angry to even feel it.

"Ye should go. Ye should see about repairing what has been done. As laird, it is ye who should speak to their laird."

When he lifted his hand again, she held up both of hers. "Don't ye dare."

Alastair grabbed her by the hair and yanked her down to her knees. "Ye will do as I tell ye."

Despite the anger, Ava knew it was best not to goad him further.

Their uncle finally spoke up. "Release yer sister. Ye cannot hope to get anything done if ye cannot control yer temper."

Properly chastised, Alastair released her and stalked back to the table and drank deeply from his tankard.

"She cannot speak to me in such a manner."

"Ava," her uncle said, looking to her. "Yer brother is now yer laird. Ye must strive to be respectful."

Two guards entered and approached. Alastair glared at Ava for a moment before acknowledging the men. "Travel to Clan Fraser. Give them the message that my uncle and sister will travel to them and arrive in two days. They come to discuss the alliance."

As the guards started to walk away, her brother spoke again. "Tell Keithen Fraser my sister will remain there. We care not in what capacity."

Ava's eyes widened. "No. Ye cannot do that. Please." She rushed to Alastair and yanked on his arm. "Call them back. Please."

When the guards left, she raced up the stairs to find her mother. If anyone could talk sense into her cruel brother, it was Lady Mackenzie. She burst into the chamber and found her mother sitting on a large settee holding a cup up to her lips accompanied by a pair of women who laughed at something she'd uttered.

Around the room, there were trays with baked tarts or goblets next to pitchers of honeyed mead.

The cool breeze blew in through windows that had been thrown open. A partially undressed young man lay stretched out on the bed. He looked to be sleeping.

A widow's life suited her mother perfectly. She'd been entertaining and enjoying different men since her father's burial.

Lady Fraser smiled warmly at her. "Come in Ava. Pour yerself some mead and join us. We are about to begin a new task."

Her mother's tasks varied from embroidery to reading a specific tome. Once, a piper was hired to teach them to play. It had been a horrendously annoying few days.

"I beg that ye speak to Alastair immediately," Ava said, looking to the bed where the young man opened his eyes and stared at her. "Who is that?" she asked, pointing to the bed.

"Our instructor," her mother said. "He is a painter. He needed rest after his long…travel."

"Mother, Alastair plans to send me to Clan Fraser."

Surprisingly, her mother immediately got to her feet. "That will not do at all." She motioned to the women. "I will return in a bit. See that Marcus eats something."

They walked down the corridor and descended the stairs to the great room, her mother's long strides making Ava rush to keep up.

"Alastair," her mother said, approaching the table where he and her uncle remained. "Ye will not send yer sister away. Those people do not deserve a Mackenzie in their midst."

"She is not a Mackenzie, but a Fraser now," Alastair replied in a bored tone. "She's married to one."

"Not by my choice," Ava interjected, even though it went without saying.

"I will not allow ye to send off yer sister to the people that rejected her so publicly."

Her brother stood, his flat gaze moving from Ava to their mother. "I am laird now, Mother, and as much as I respect yer opinion, I must do what is best for our clan. Did Father not say it matters not who pays as long as we gain power?"

Lady Mackenzie stilled, seeming to see that Alastair was not at all different than her newly departed husband. "He did."

As much as Ava had hoped her intervention would help, she began to lose hope.

"I fear yer brother is correct," her mother uttered. "Ye are a Fraser now. We must do what is best for our clan."

It was as if the room swayed and she grabbed the back of a chair. She was a woman without a family, without a clan and without any claim.

Unwanted by her family and her husband.

CHAPTER NINE

KEITHEN ENTERED THE study and immediately every eye turned to him. His father looked particularly discomfited and cleared his throat.

When no one spoke, he didn't ask what had happened. Obviously, it had to do with him and perhaps it was time to tell the truth. Time to confess that he'd been the one who'd been killing the guardsmen who'd attacked Catriona. However, as much as he admired who did it, he could not take responsibility, or perhaps credit, for Laird Mackenzie's death.

"I did not kill Laird Mackenzie," Keithen said, starting what he was sure would be a long period of questioning. "Whoever did must have had a greater quarrel with the man. When we find out who it is, we should invite him over to celebrate with us."

His father motioned for him to sit. "It is not known who killed Laird Mackenzie. I am glad to hear it was not ye."

"Of course, they will wish to blame us. I suppose we should prepare for war," Keithen replied.

"Although they have become smaller in size, we do not wish to head into battle," a council member added.

Broden gave Keithen a pointed look. "They've sent a messenger. The man was just sent to the kitchen to seek a meal."

What could Alastair Mackenzie want so soon? "If he wishes to visit, I suggest we deny him."

"It is not he who comes," his father started.

"Does it matter?" Keithen interrupted. "After everything they did, why would they seek to come here? We do not owe them any kind of favor."

"Stop speaking and listen," Broden snapped. "Unlike the other lairds, we could not break our alliance with them for obvious reasons."

The marriage of course. He and Ava Mackenzie were married and, therefore, the two clans remained bound.

Laird Fraser stood to his full height. Although a bit shorter than Keithen, his father was not a small man. Of slim build, he remained in good form.

"A Mackenzie, I believe brother to the late laird is who comes. I believe they plan to discuss our alliance and seek to ensure it remains strong."

"Have we a choice?" Keithen asked.

"Although we will remain allied to Clan Mackenzie, there will be no sworn fealty between us. Despite the fact they send a pawn."

"A pawn?" Keithen glared toward the doorway. Was there no way to ever get rid of the albatross that was Clan Mackenzie? Almost every other allied clan except for them had broken their ties immediately upon the laird's passing. It was only those that were bound by marriages that remained.

"…to live here." Keithen wasn't sure what he'd missed. He'd been too busy musing about the inconvenience of the situation. Admittedly, they did not have to fear another thrashing as the clan was much smaller now.

"What did ye say?" he asked his father, noting everyone seemed to be awaiting his reaction.

"Yer wife is being brought to live here." His father locked gazes with him. "They say she is not a Mackenzie but a Fraser."

TWO DAYS LATER, a carriage flanked by four horsemen, which was followed by a contingent of twenty warriors, entered through the gates.

Along with his parents, Keithen stood at the entrance to the home waiting for the visitors to appear.

This had to be so very hard for Ava to be sent back to the husband who'd rejected her. Of course, there was a reason for it, in which Ava had no choice in the matter.

First, two horsemen dismounted. One walked toward them and handed his father a missive. "My laird sends his regards and thanks ye for yer hospitality."

His father nodded in response, his gaze moving to the carriage. The door opened and an older man emerged. Dressed neutrally, he did not don the Mackenzie colors. With silvered sideburns and hair that was pulled back into a queue, he seemed more English than Scottish.

The man held out an arm and from the carriage emerged an older woman, obviously his wife. She was dressed much like Keithen's mother in a gown of muted tones.

Finally, Ava appeared. With her dark hair pulled back and swept up, she looked refined and composed. Her dark blue skirts flowed out behind her as she stepped down from the carriage. Across her shoulders she wore a shawl in a dark shade of green. A subtle nod to the Mackenzie colors.

The older couple and Ava walked toward them and Keithen could not keep from admiring his proud wife. Her gaze remained forward, chin up and shoulders back. There was a serenity about her, as if she were some sort of fabled creature, untouchable and beautiful.

"Greet yer wife," his mother prodded, bringing him out of being struck silent by her appearance.

Keithen stepped forward and held out his arm. "Wife."

For a long moment, he did not think she'd accept it. But after a moment's hesitation, she placed her hand on the crook of his arm. "Husband." Her voice was husky and velvety. He remembered the tone of it long after seeing her for what he thought was the last time.

Unlike the last time, this time she would remain with him as he vowed to never humiliate her by rejecting her again. If he did, as she'd been pronounced no longer a "Mackenzie", she would have nowhere to go.

They turned and waited for her uncle to introduce himself and his wife. Once that was done, the group went inside.

The visitors were escorted to a rarely used dining room that was reserved for family meals. Since they usually ate in the great room, this room was saved mainly for special visitors.

Brandy was poured for everyone and trays of bread, cheese and a tart of poached pears were set out. Ava's aunt and uncle, Liam and Theresa Mackenzie, were pleasant. Although Liam maintained a cool demeanor, his intelligent gaze seemed to take in every nuance.

The woman, Theresa, praised the room's décor and began to ask his mother questions about the garden she'd managed to sneak a peek of somehow.

The entire time, Ava remained quiet. Other than taking a sip of the brandy that was placed in front of her, she did not eat.

Keithen was at a loss as to what to say to her. It wasn't as if any kind of pleasant conversation would set either of them at ease.

"Ava, do ye like pears?" his mother asked. "They are poached with honey before being placed in the tart."

His wife's face paled and she swallowed visibly. It became apparent that the poor woman's emotions were barely held in check. "I do."

When his mother looked to him and then to the tartlet, he cut a slice, slid it on a plate and placed it in front of her.

"Are ye to be living at the keep now that yer brother has

gone?" his father asked the visiting man.

"No, we live in the south still on Mackenzie lands. We have a large estate there. I prefer the southern area. It is much warmer. The weather here is much too frigid."

Keithen met his father's gaze. Did these people travel for two days to speak of the weather?

The man's lips curved. "If I may be so bold as to explain our presence. We come to escort Ava as we will continue on our travel home. We've spent the last month visiting with my brother's family after his passing."

"I was led to believe there was another reason for yer visit," his father said. It was not courteous to do so, but being that the two clans were not on friendly terms, there was no need to mince words.

Liam Mackenzie nodded. "My nephew wishes to strengthen the bonds of yer alliance. That, I believe, is why we are here to deposit Ava."

At the words, Ava looked to her uncle, but did not speak.

"A true alliance is not made through force," Keithen said, "but by mutual agreement. Although we are bound to yer nephew by our marriage, know that we will never fight alongside him, nor will we defend him if called upon."

The man did not act surprised at the words. "I understand my late brother was not well liked. However, the alliance is not broken. Therefore, ye will be held to certain expectations."

Laird Fraser tapped the table with his fingertips. "We should continue this discussion after last meal. I am sure the women are weary from travel."

Lady Fraser rose. "I will show ye to the chambers I had prepared. I know ye will be comfortable there." She gave Keithen a pointed look. "Keithen, ensure Ava is settled in yer chamber."

As her parents led the visitors out, Keithen also stood and took Ava's elbow. "If I know my mother, yer baggage is already deposited in our chamber."

Her brow crinkled as if not liking what was said, but she

didn't say anything. Instead, she turned to look to the doorway, and it was then he noticed a dark bruise on her left temple that ran to her cheek.

"What happened to yer face?"

Her hand flew to the precise spot and she covered it. "Nothing that should concern ye."

Keithen stepped in front of her. "Who struck ye?"

Once again, it was apparent that she was struggling to maintain a calm demeanor. Her eyes filled with tears and she lowered her head. "I caused it because I spoke out of turn. Will ye please escort me to the bedchamber? I require some rest."

He knew better. The woman had ridden nonstop for an entire day just to purchase fruit tarts. However, she was humiliated twice now. First, rejected by him and sent back to live with her family and now, sent back.

The tightness in his chest became stronger when he noticed a slight tremble of her chin.

"Aye, of course. Ye can spend the rest of the day relaxing. If ye wish to have a chambermaid assist with unpacking, I can have one attend to it." Keithen spoke of nothing more than unpacking, having fresh water bought and such the entire way to their bedchamber.

Two things struck him at once, and it was becoming impossible to ignore either. First, that he would do anything in his power to keep Ava from crying. The woman who walked beside him was one of the strongest people he'd ever met and to see her so broken struck him to the core. Second, his wife was there and would not only be living in the same house, but they'd be sharing a bed from that night forward.

To send her away to sleep elsewhere at that point would be another horrible strike and he would not do it.

When they entered the chamber, true to form, her bags were there and several of her gowns were already unpacked and hung in the wardrobe. Keithen was struck by the sight of the dresses hanging next to his tunics.

Ava looked about the room in which she'd only spent one night. Their wedding night in which Keithen had claimed her as his bride.

Not seeming interested in her bags, she went to the window and peered out. He knew what she saw. To the left were rolling hills, a long winding road and, in the distance, the edges of the village. Straight ahead was an open field that was used for training with the warhorses and large gatherings. Then past the open area was a thick forest that stretched as far as the eye could see. Just behind the keep was another forest and a shallow creek that was used for drinking water and the watering of the gardens.

There were several farms as well, but most were not visible unless one stood on the rooftop.

Keithen studied Ava's profile for a long moment. "Despite the circumstances, I am glad ye are here."

It was apparent she didn't believe him by her flat gaze. "I am not sure what to say."

"My mother will wish to spend time with ye and go over what duties ye will be taking over."

At her surprised look, Keithen shrugged. "She assured me she is looking forward to having some of her duties taken over by ye. Since my sister left, her time is much less hers."

Ava nodded. "Do ye know what kind of duties she will give me? I have managed most of my household, therefore I'm competent."

"I do not know but I am sure she will explain it to ye."

There was uncertainty when she looked to him. "Surely yer mother expected someone else as yer wife, not me, a Mackenzie."

"Mother is a kind person, I assure ye. She does not harbor any rancor toward ye."

When Ava wrung her hands, he wanted to calm her, but wasn't sure how to go about it. "I am not sure yer household will allow for a Mackenzie to give any orders."

"I will ensure they do," Keithen said, knowing it would be a hard road ahead for Ava. Wounds were still fresh, and people did not forget that it was a Mackenzie who'd taken so many brothers, fathers and sons from them.

Her right eyebrow rose, giving a hint of the spitfire he remembered. "And how, exactly, do ye plan to arrange for the staff to fall in line and do as I ask?"

Keithen fought not to smile. "At first, I will speak to them. If that does not work, I will threaten them."

"What is yer mother like?"

At the question, he had to consider how Lady Fraser came across. "Mother is spirited and at the same time calm. She manages to make time for whatever requires her attention. As much as she comes and goes, I often wonder how she ensures the house is run so well. Our staff respects and likes her. Through the years, she somehow was able to keep Esme and me from killing each other."

Ava studied him for a long moment. "Does she hold influence over yer father?"

It was a strange question. But then he considered that her father was ruthless and perhaps Lady Mackenzie was as well. "She does, in a way. They balance each other well."

When she frowned and turned away, he knew Ava's mind was in all probability going over what her life would be like.

"Ye should rest now. I will return later."

CHAPTER TEN

HER FIRST MEAL at Fraser Keep went exactly as Ava expected. When people thought the laird's family didn't notice, they glared at her. Occasionally, she caught women looking from her to Keithen with obvious contempt.

Admittedly, her husband was quite handsome, which made her wonder how many of the women in the room had hoped for marriage. She slid a look to him as trays laden with freshly sliced meat were placed on the table.

"I expect it will get better over time." Although he kept his gaze forward, he'd caught her looking at him. "Ye will have to be patient."

Patience was the one thing she was exhausted of. For years, she'd been ignored by her family and late husband. At last meals, she'd grown accustomed to eating quickly and leaving since it was rare that anyone deemed it necessary for her to be part of any conversation.

Now again, this time, she had to wait and allow the people in the room, that would sooner see her dead, to not hate her. Ava almost laughed at the thought. "My life has been a study in patience," she replied.

Without asking, Keithen served her. Taking time to choose

the best cuts, he placed two pieces of meat on her plate. Then he once again took great pains to choose pieces of chopped turnip and did the same.

Ava wasn't sure what to think of the practice. She'd not noticed any of the other husbands doing the same for their wives. Then again, she'd been much too busy trying to avoid eye contact while keeping her head up.

Instinctively, she knew it was imperative not to show weakness.

Seeming oblivious to the lukewarm reception by the others in the room, her aunt and Lady Fraser acted as if they were long-lost friends. Their conversation continuing about gardening and managing a large household. Lady Fraser, who sat on the other side of the laird, leaned forward to speak over the woman's husband, until he finally ceded his seat to her.

When the meal was over, Ava allowed Keithen to help her to her feet, unsure what she'd do next.

He guided her to a table where two women sat, one that she immediately recognized as Catriona, the other a pleasant woman who smiled up at her warmly.

"Please sit," Catriona invited. "I hope yer first meal here was not too unpleasant." The woman looked to Keithen and a kind of unspoken exchange happened between them.

As the people in the room dispersed, most to find their way home, the room became almost empty. She noted that a few people lingered, almost reluctant to leave, some chatting amiably with guards, others with the laird and his wife.

The difference between life in this keep and her own was astounding. Unless putting up a front for visiting lairds, people from the surrounding villages were never invited to share last meal. And when they did come, there was a strained atmosphere as most were afraid to do anything that would annoy her late father.

When laughter sounded, Ava started, unused to hearing it inside. Two men bent at the waist laughing so hard, they wiped tears from their faces. Keithen neared and they tried to tell him what they spoke of but had a hard time as they could not contain their mirth. Finally, Keithen joined in the laughter, producing a deep rich sound.

"It is quite different here than what I am used to," Ava admitted when she noticed Catriona and the other woman studying her. "There was never laughter in my home."

"I cannot imagine life without the sound of it," the woman said. "I am Flora, Miss Catriona's companion."

Ava met the woman's gaze and understood the silent message. Catriona remained fragile and she should proceed with caution when discussing anything to do with her home or clan.

Thankfully, Catriona didn't seem to notice. She gave Ava's hand a soft squeeze. "How do ye feel?"

After what the woman had been through, tossed to guards by her father to do with as they saw fit, which they did, Ava was struck by her kindness.

"As if in a dream. Not a good dream at that," Ava confided. "I am not sure how to feel actually."

Catriona's gaze moved from her to where Keithen stood. "He is a good and honorable man who will stand by ye. Believe me when I tell ye that it was not easy for him to send ye away."

A familiar tightness in her chest formed at the reminder of one of the most humiliating days of her life.

"Lady Fraser has invited us to picnic in the garden tomorrow," her aunt announced, having neared. "I am afraid this day has proven too much and I must retire."

Ava stood and kissed her aunt's cheek. "Thank ye for coming, Aunt Theresa. Yer presence means so much to me."

Her aunt nodded in understanding. "I worry for ye, sweet dear. It will be hard to leave ye here. However, I will have to trust that yer husband will keep ye safe."

Both looked to where Keithen and the two men remained. All three were in deep conversation with gesturing and such. It looked as if they were close friends.

When she sat, Catriona too looked to where the men were. "The man on the left is Ewan Ross, cousin to Laird Malcolm Ross. He, along with fifty men, came to live here after our alliance with his clan. The other is Broden McRainey, a guard and childhood friend of Keithen's."

"Yer clan and Clan Ross have become very close," Ava stated matter-of-factly. "Tis nice when those things happen on friendly terms."

"Aye," Catriona agreed. "I plan to visit, once I am able to travel…I miss Esme greatly."

Esme Ross had married a cousin to Laird Ross, Ruari, a man Ava had met once. She had been struck by the man's large physique.

It was not much later that Keithen came to fetch her. Obviously, he'd noticed her yawning. Catriona and Flora stood and also claimed to be retiring.

Altogether, by the end of the evening, Ava had not had a totally unpleasant day. Ending the evening in the company of women had not been something she was used it and she had struggled to maintain a conversation. Thankfully, Catriona seemed to not mind long moments of silence.

THE BEDCHAMBER HAD been prepared for them. Obviously, someone had ordered fresh bedding and for the fire to be lit. There was a pitcher of flowers on a table and neatly folded cloths on the wash basin.

Unsure how to proceed, Ava moved to stand in front of the fire and held out her hands although, if she were to be honest, it wasn't necessary.

"I will give ye privacy to prepare for bed," Keithen said and walked out of the room.

It wasn't going to be that way between them for long, she was aware. However, it was very kind of him to allow it then. Ava hurriedly undressed and with the water and a fragrant poultice that were on the washstand, cleansed away the dirt of the day. Once done, she slipped a night rail on over her head and climbed into the bed.

Not much later, Keithen entered. He didn't look toward the bed, but instead went to the wardrobe and removed his boots and trews. She noted he left his tunic on and then, like her, washed up at the washstand.

Then he climbed into bed and lay on his back looking up at the ceiling.

"I am not used to sharing my bedchamber…or my bed actually," he said, still looking straight up. "If I do something while I'm asleep that annoys ye, do not hesitate to jab me with yer elbow."

Ava turned to gape at him. "Jab ye?"

"Ye know," he demonstrated by gently pushing his elbow into her side. "To wake me."

She considered it for a long moment. The conversation was not what she'd expected. "Do ye keep a dirk under yer pillow? What if ye think I am an intruder?"

"Good point." He slid from the bed, reached under his pillow and pulled out not one, but two blades. Then he walked to the fireplace and put them on the mantel.

Ava lay on her back and met his gaze. If they were to have relations, she prepared herself mentally and was as ready as one could be for the cumbersome activity. "Can ye douse the light please?"

"Aye, of course." The room was instantly darker. However, there was a bright moon and so she could still make him out.

He climbed into the bed and let out a loud yawn. "Sleep well."

Her husband turned on his side, the wideness of his back blocking her view of the doorway.

"Good…night," Ava finally replied, unsure what was transpiring. She was about to poke him in the back with a finger and ask if she should do something, but the sound of a soft snore stopped her.

WHEN MORNING CAME, Ava sighed, not wanting to wake. It was so very warm in the cocoon she'd made for herself. The softness of the bedding as well as the firm structure she was pressed against made for a perfect restful morning. And then her eyes flew wide.

Not only was she in a strange place, but she was firmly pressed against her husband's side.

She wiggled away from him and pressed her face into the pillow to keep quiet as she gasped for air. Thankfully, he seemed to continue to sleep.

When her breathing regulated, she looked toward Keithen through slitted eyes. He was on his back, one arm over his head, the other across his midsection. The blankets had slipped just past his chest and his tunic had ridden halfway up his chest. There was a sprinkling of hair that trickled down the center of it.

Several bumpy scars, one recent, reddened his otherwise smooth skin.

Soft breathing from his parted lips and the rising and falling of his chest took her attention for a long time. He slept rather late for a warrior, Ava considered. By light from the window, it was still early. However, at her keep, warriors had to be up and on duty by dawn.

It was rather silly, now that she considered it. Another of her father's strange rules that made little sense as the sleepy men rarely looked fit to defend anyone.

After slipping from the bed, Ava dressed and then went to the window. She wasn't brave enough to leave the room alone and even if she did, it was a house she was not familiar with.

Today, she'd ask Keithen to take her to the kitchen. Hopefully, if she offered to help, she could find an ally in the cook. The only people she felt comfortable with and spent time talking to back at her keep had been the kitchen maids, who'd grown used to her mingling there when having nothing else to do.

Keithen woke with a yawn and stretched. He looked around the room with a scowl, but upon seeing her, his expression relaxed.

Moments later, there was a knock on the door. Keithen called out for whoever it was to enter.

A young maid walked in with a tray and greeted them. "Lady Fraser asked that I bring warm cider for ye," she said, looking to Ava. "Mister Keithen, yer father requests yer presence before first meal."

"Yer mother is very kind," Ava said as she lifted the cup to her lips.

Keithen nodded and slid from the bed. "Aye, she is. Ye will find an ally in her. Upon her marriage to my father, her clan and ours were not on the best of terms. Not as much so as with yers, but it was not a friendly union."

"Should I come down with ye?"

As he wrapped a belt around his waist and then proceeded to pull his boots on, Keithen pondered her question.

"I will ask a servant to fetch ye for first meal. Or perhaps my mother already plans to come for ye herself."

When he left the room, Ava paced. This was the most surreal experience of her life. What was to happen next?'

Was it possible that for the first time in her life, she was to have a somewhat normal life? "Goodness," she said out loud, returning to the window to study what was happening in the courtyard.

Outside, people mingled and, once again, she was struck by the serenity of it. Hopefully one day, she'd be able to walk about the courtyard without being seen as an outsider.

CHAPTER ELEVEN

FOR FOUR LONG nights, Keithen had been in the bed next to Ava and, each night, he'd fought every instinct to take her. She was his wife, after all. However, he couldn't bring himself to see past what she represented, who she was.

A Mackenzie lay in his bed, next to him nightly now.

Her people had destroyed Catriona, a woman he'd cherished, spent time with as a child. The one person he'd shared every one of his childhood secrets with. Then, as adults, they'd remained confidantes and friends.

How could he now take the woman he craved with every inch of his being without feeling as if he betrayed the other.

The light from the lantern illuminated her façade as she stood just outside the window on the balcony. Every night, she spent long moments looking up at the sky. Every so often, she'd remark on seeing a shooting star or on certain patterns in the skies.

Her serenity brought him calm after long days. At the same time, he was aware she was suffering. His mother had kept him informed of what was happening while he was gone out on patrol.

How Ava's offers to help in the kitchen had been refused and when she'd tried to hand out duties to the chambermaids, they'd pretended not to hear her.

As much as he wanted to step in, what happened with the servants and household was firmly his mother's jurisdiction. Lady Fraser had told him that under no circumstances must he interfere. If Ava were to be accepted, it would have to be between Ava and the staff.

A cold breeze blew in and he picked up her shawl and walked out to the balcony. Below, there was a bonfire and musicians played a lively tune that traveled up to where they stood.

"What do they celebrate?" Ava asked, accepting the shawl. "There seems to be a lot of joviality here."

Keithen looked down and smiled. Broden was attempting to tempt a young lass away from the group. "Travelers from the south, returning home. They asked to camp here so they would be protected."

"Does it happen often?"

He studied her for a long moment. "At times, it seems we have lived very different lives. Does it not?"

When she blinked, he wasn't sure if it was tears or just the breeze causing it. "We have. I do not remember any travelers ever asking for our hospitality."

Of course not. The Mackenzie wasn't known for being kind. Keithen refrained from saying what he was thinking. "It happens about every fortnight or so. Not as much during the winter when it is a bother because we have to host them indoors, and it can get quite crowded."

There was a soft expression on her face when she looked at him. When she looked back to the people, there was a soft lift to the corners of her lips. "It is nice."

"It is." Keithen came up to her and pulled her into an embrace. "I wish ye would have had a better life."

At first, she stiffened. But then she relaxed against him. For a long moment, they stood with her back against his chest, listening to the playful melodies from below.

The woman was his to take and, yet, Keithen wouldn't do so

without her being willing. He pressed a kiss to the side of her neck and wrapped his arms tighter around her waist.

When she sighed and slid a hand down his arm, permission was granted, and his body instantly reacted. Blood surged through him, sending tendrils of awareness to every part of his being.

For the first time in his life, Keithen wasn't entirely sure how to proceed. This woman was to be his for the rest of their existence.

This night could be the first of many making love.

Ava turned in his arms and peered up at him. "We've never kissed."

"Aye, we did," Keithen replied. "Once." Although the marriage kiss had been more of a peck.

He took her mouth then, testing and savoring the plump pillowy offerings. Her breaths intermingled with his as she began to respond.

Emboldened, he cupped her face and slid his tongue along the crease of her mouth and then nibbled at each corner. She tasted sweet, her usual late evening cider lingering. When he repeated the gesture, Keithen whispered, "Open yer lips for me."

She did as he instructed, her lips parting, and he slid his tongue into her mouth. The beauty trembled in his arms and pushed her own tongue against his.

Through the thin fabric of her night rail, he could feel the warmth of Ava's skin as his palms roved down the mounds of her bottom.

Once again, she shook, and he wondered how it had been possible to keep away from her for so long.

Needing to see her, he pushed away and tugged at the string tied at her neck. The flimsy fabric gave way as he pushed it off her shoulders. It slid down every tantalizing inch of her body and finally pooled around her feet.

She didn't shy away, nor did she try to cover up. Instead, she studied him intently in return. Ava was exquisite, her plush body made to drive a man mad with passion.

"Ye are beautiful," he finally said, feeling like a tongue-tied lad. "Perfect."

Ava seemed at a loss for what to do, so he closed the distance between them and lifted her up and then placed her on the bed.

She lay awkwardly without moving, her gaze up at the ceiling.

Keithen undressed and climbed onto the bed. "Tis not a duty that ye allow me to take ye. I wish it to be pleasurable for the both of us."

"I do not understand."

"Did ye not enjoy our kissing?"

"Aye, I did." A soft pink appeared on her cheeks. "Very much."

"How about when I touched ye?" He placed a hand on her hip and caressed the soft skin.

This time, she nodded as a reply.

"I have been bedded before by my late husband. And yet, it wasn't very enjoyable," Ava admitted. "What I felt when we kiss, it was never like with ye, just now."

"Because he was only interested in his own pleasure. Allow me will show ye what it is to make love, so that we both derive pleasure from it."

He took her hand. "Come. Slide up here."

They moved together to lay side by side on the bed.

If he were to be honest, teaching her to make love was proving to be quite enjoyable. He was already hard, but Keithen took a breath, reminding himself he would have to take things slow.

He pulled her into his arms and began to kiss her again. While they kissed, he pulled her against him and caressed her arms, side and hips.

Then he began trailing his lips down her neck and shoulders. A soft moan escaped her lips when his mouth took in a pink tip of her breast while he strummed the other with the pad of his thumb.

Satisfaction roared when her fingers interlaced in his hair. Keithen didn't stop suckling her breasts, moving from one to the other until she began to shift her hips.

Then he slid a hand down from her stomach to between her legs.

At first, she stiffened. But when he found the center and circled it with his fingers, she soon became lost.

"That's it. Enjoy it," Keithen said and then took her mouth with his once again.

Ava orgasmed into his hand, the walls of her sex quivering and she cried out as she dug her fingernails into his shoulders.

His cock throbbed, demanding that he take her fully. But first he waited for her to settle.

Lithe and limber, she opened her eyes and looked at him with a shocked expression. "What was that?"

"Pleasure," he replied, his mouth on hers again. She reciprocated with enthusiasm, this time, giving as much as he did. Her mouth accepting every inch of his tongue which she suckled.

When he settled between her legs and slid up and down, allowing his member to glide between her folds, Ava arched her back. The friction of their bodies was almost the end for him, but Keithen blew out breaths and concentrated on how amazing it would feel to finally enter her.

Taking himself in hand, he guided himself to her entrance. She was hot, wet and ready to accept him.

He pushed into her, inch-by-inch until fully sheathed. Ava tightened around him. He stilled to allow her sex to accommodate his girth.

"Relax," he whispered into Ava's ear. "Allow yerself to enjoy this, as well."

Although there was doubt in her expression, she finally began to relax.

Keeping still, he studied the beauty beneath him. Her hair was splayed across the bedding, her full breasts moved up and down with each breath.

Finally, he inched out just a bit and pushed back in. He repeated it and then again.

Ava began to keep up with the rhythm of his movements. Encouraged by her desire, he was driving in and out of her with vigor.

Fiery trails blazed from his extremities until pooling in his center and exploding out with so much force that Keithen thought he'd certainly pass out. He shuddered in release, his body quaking as his eyes rolled and he could no longer keep from collapsing over Ava.

She'd cried out perhaps, he wasn't sure. But like him, she trembled and moaned, her sex constricting around his cock and then she seemed to melt into the bedding.

"I cannot move. I do apologize," Keithen mumbled.

"Mmmm," Ava replied.

KEITHEN WOKE WITH a start and turned to find that he was alone in bed. The sun's rays coming through the window made the room brighter than usual. That told him that he'd overslept. Thoughts of the night before made him fall back onto the bed. What transpired between him and Ava the night before had been so different than any other sexual experience. It was as if they'd become joined more than just physically.

"I'm going mad," he mumbled as he got up from the bed. It had to be that he'd gone too long without bedding a woman. Or. He stopped and looked to the bed. Mayhap, it was that the marriage bond made intimacy something more than just their bodies.

His wife emerged from behind the screen in the corner, fully dressed. Upon seeing him, her cheeks turned pick. "Good morning, Husband."

Their gazes held while he slid from the bed. "Good morning, Ava."

"THERE IS SMOKE in the distance." Ewan Ross pointed north as they patrolled the area of the land near their border with Mackenzie lands. So far, since the laird's passing, Clan Mackenzie had been quiet.

The sense among the lairds was that Alastair Mackenzie was learning his way but would eventually be as untrustworthy as his father. Except for perhaps the Sutherland, the lairds kept their distance while keeping watchful eyes on the volatile clan.

"The harvest is not done, so it makes little sense for anyone to burn fields," Keithen said. "We should go see about it." He turned to Broden and another guard who rode behind them. "Return and inform my father that Ewan and I are going into Mackenzie lands to investigate what is going on with the distant smoke. Do not tell anyone else."

The men did as they were told and rode off.

Urging their horses to a gallop, they rode for several hours before stopping at the site of Mackenzie Keep under siege.

"Who is attacking?" Ewan asked and narrowed his eyes to get a better look. "I do not see any colors displayed."

Gallant, Keithen's horse, pawed the ground. The animal sensed war and expected they'd be joining.

"It is getting too dark to see. If I were to guess, I would say the MacDonnells. They've been waiting for this opportunity after their villages were burned to the ground."

The sounds of war carried to where they stood. No one would come to the Mackenzies' aid except for perhaps the other Laird Mackenzie to the north, who was much too far away to arrive promptly.

"Do ye think they will send a messenger to request our help?" Ewan asked.

"Aye, they probably already have."

Gallant neighed and kicked up his huge hooves, alerting them that riders were approaching. Keithen drew his sword, noting that Ewan did as well.

Four riders came near with swords drawn. They were Mackenzies. "Why do ye lurk about our lands?" one of them said with a sneer. He motioned toward the keep. "Unless, this is yer doing?"

"What would we have to gain?" Keithen replied, pulling back on his horse to keep it from charging.

The men exchanged looks and one spit on the ground. "Nothing good comes from a Fraser. Ye have been wishing for revenge. We know it is one of ye that has been killing our guardsmen."

Rage surged through Keithen's veins, but he managed not to show it. "Perhaps yer guards needed to spend more time training?"

The men charged, swords clanging as each swung against the other. Keithen and Ewan each fought two, which proved unfortunate. Although he'd face similar odds several times and Keithen knew how he had to block one while striking toward the other, within minutes, he was becoming winded.

Thankfully, Gallant managed to crush one of the men's legs, which gave Keithen a bit of a reprieve.

One of Ewan's opponents fell to the ground, but both of Keithen's continued to fight. He held up a short sword with his left arm, just as the man sliced across, the blade cutting through his sleeve and into this skin.

"Augh!" Keithen growled and managed to turn in time to block a strike from the other side.

Suddenly, a rider came through the woods. On a fast and lithe horse, the masked rider circled them, disconcerting the fighters who tried to figure out which side would have a new advantage.

When one of the men Keithen fought fell to the ground from a strike of the masked man's sword, Keithen took advantage and fought against the other one left.

He managed to throw the man off balance before striking him down. The one who'd fallen on the ground now fought with the masked rider. Ewan and his opponent continued to fight as well.

Finally, the masked rider overcame the one on the ground and Ewan's opponent fled into the forest.

"If he goes to the Mackenzie, they may declare war on yer clan," Ewan said, looking to Keithen. "Should we go after him?"

"No. They have enough on their hands. I doubt the idiot will come after us. We are evenly matched now. We may even have an advantage after this battle."

"Who are ye?" Keithen turned to see that the masked rider was riding away.

He and Ewan exchanged looks. "Have ye seen him before?" Ewan asked.

Keithen nodded. "Aye, once. Almost the same place. He must be someone who lives near here. Whoever it is seems to take sides against the Mackenzies."

They dismounted so that Keithen could wrap his injured arm. After a cursory check on the horses to ensure they were not injured, they rode closer to Mackenzie Keep to find out exactly who had attacked.

From the lack of activity, the battle was ending. The falling sun and long shadows made it almost impossible to distinguish between enemy and ally.

A torch illuminated a banner that was lifted as men called out chants. It was, indeed, the MacDonnells who'd attacked.

The walls had not been breached and yet both sides had suffered causalities. Neither side had won and yet it had been enough of a warning to the Mackenzie from the opposing clan that they were not to be toyed with.

If Keithen were to guess, the lack of support from local clans also sent a hard message to the new laird. They were without allies. That was a direct result of their past misdeeds.

Riding back to the keep, Keithen cradled his arm against his body. The cut, which was on the forearm, throbbed. His left side ached from a strike and he was sure there was another injury on his right shoulder.

He studied Ewan's bloody tunic. "The healer will be busy tonight. This is not yer fight. I should have asked ye to return to the keep and not Broden."

Ewan shrugged good-naturedly. "I was becoming bored. Tonight got my blood flowing. Tis good to keep the sword arm in good use."

"Ye're a good swordsman. Ye must have spent a lot of time training." Keithen left out the part acknowledging that where Ewan grew up, there was rarely any threat or need for fighting knowledge. The people of Uist were separated from Scotland by water and, therefore, it would be hard to overtake them unless the attackers had a large fleet of birlinns to traverse the uncertain waters.

The man was a contradiction. While he was easygoing, he was still a fierce warrior. He was large in size, but often played with children in the courtyard like an oversized lad.

"Do ye plan to return to Ross Keep in the spring?" Keithen asked, truly curious.

Once again, Ewan shrugged. "I may return to Uist. I have not decided as of yet. I came here to find my true calling. My father and brother have things well in hand back home, when it comes to caring for the people and lands. My sole responsibility was to be a guard."

"Not much different than here," Keithen said.

"Not true." Ewan looked up to the sky. "There was rarely an opportunity to engage in battle in Uist."

"Battling and threats can be exhausting. People get hurt or die."

Ewan nodded understanding. "Aye, there is that. However, I cannot understand a life without true purpose."

Keithen understood. His own path was set. One day, he'd be laird and be responsible for the people on the land surrounding his home. He would raise a family there at Fraser Keep and would spend days tending to the needs of the people, meeting with other lairds and maintaining control of the borders. He had a purpose, which he relished. It was hard to imagine Ewan's status. Or lack thereof.

IT WAS NEARLY dawn when Keithen and Ewan finally entered the courtyard where everything was just as when they'd left.

Once they dismounted and the horses given over to the stable lads, he and Ewan made their way into the main house.

His mother rushed to him. "What happened? Ye're injured."

"I will live," Keithen assured her, pressing a kiss to her cheek. "However, we both require the healer."

Catriona came to him and looked first at his arm and then to Ewan. She quickly looked away when meeting gazes with Ewan.

"Come, I will wash out yer injuries while the healer is summoned."

They followed the woman to the back of the great room and sat at a table. Bowls of water and cloths were brought. Both he and Ewan's tunics were cut away and what looked to be an army of servants began to clean the cuts and press compresses into bruises. Keithen frowned, noting his mother hovering and ordering for this and that to be brought.

"Mother. All I require is for my cuts to be stitched and some rest. I assure ye other than being very sleepy, I am fine."

Her gaze roved over him, and she pinpointed an angry gash on his shoulder. "Remain still. The healer comes soon."

"What happened last night?" he finally asked Catriona. "Why is Mother acting so overprotective?"

"A messenger arrived to inform us that yer cousin, Blair, died in an ambush. She was most alarmed when yer messenger arrived just moments later."

He'd find out later from his father who'd killed his cousin. The other Clan Fraser was larger than theirs and whoever did it would be made to pay.

Just then, Ava appeared at the top of the stairs. She looked in his direction and hurried down. As she approached, he noted, she looked tired. Had she been up worrying about him, as well?

There was a calmness in her gaze when it traveled from his face down to the two wounds. "I will see to his wounds," Ava said, taking a cloth from a servant. "Please bring whisky, needle and thread."

Moments later, he was laid onto the table. Ava placed a clean cloth over his chest and crossed his left arm atop it. "This will burn a bit." She poured whisky into the wound.

It hurt. Keithen gritted his teeth. "What are ye doing?"

"Ensuring it doesn't fester," she replied calmly and then dipped the needle in the whisky. Each stitch burned. Keithen was glad when the last one was completed.

Once she finished with his arm, she did the same to his left shoulder which, thankfully, had only a small cut.

With quick moves, she mixed several items to make a poultice that was placed on his bruises. Then she examined Ewan and also cleaned his cuts and sewed one shut.

By the time she was done, they were bandaged in clean cloths and fed a light stew.

She walked beside him up to the bedroom and sat on the bed when he laid upon it. "I am glad to see ye are not hurt too badly. Yer mother was very worried."

The way his wife hovered made him wonder if she was worried, as well. "Thank ye for caring for my wounds. Ye are quite good at it."

"I studied healing," she replied, her gaze meeting his. "It felt good to be needed."

Unable to help it, Keithen yawned and lifted up to place a kiss to her lips.

Ava slipped from the bed and lowered to a chair. She lifted an embroidery hoop and studied her work.

Just as his eyes closed, Keithen saw something that looked to be a bruise just under the cuff of her sleeve.

"What happened…" his words slurred as he spoke.

"What?"

"The bruise…"

Ava pressed her lips together. "Rest."

He'd have to ask her later. At the moment, whatever she'd given him pulled him to a deep slumber.

The touch of a hand on his face could have been his imagination, but it felt so real.

CHAPTER TWELVE

THERE WERE SEVERAL places at Fraser Keep that Ava could go without the glares of either servants or villagers. Her days were spent between her bedchamber, Lady Fraser's sitting room and a new garden she'd begun working on. The long hours tilling the dark earth and preparing it for planting gave her purpose. Although she'd not be able to plant anything for a long time, it would be ready when the snow melted in the spring.

Ava would plant herbs and a variety of plants with healing properties. She hoped to convince Keithen to go with her into the forest to forage for the necessary plants.

A woman came around the corner and watched her. Ava pretended not to notice, but caught a glimpse of the skirts.

"Ye are doing well here," Flora said. The village woman who cared for Catriona neared. "This area may not receive enough sunlight for plants to thrive."

Ava smiled. "There is afternoon sun here, which I think lasts longer than morning sun."

The woman watched her for a few moments. "I was very angry when ye first came here. I did my best not to be because what yer father did was not yer fault. But still, I did not like ye."

Not sure what to say, Ava kneeled and began digging with

her spade. Tears threatened to overflow. Why could she not become accustomed to being an outcast? She was unwanted wherever she went.

When a droplet hit the back of her hand, she took a breath. "I do not expect anyone to care for me. But I do hope that someday ye and the others will be kind."

Flora lowered to sit on a small stool. "I cannot imagine what it is like here for ye and must admit to admiring how ye carry on."

"What choice do I have?" Ava replied with a sniff. "It is my lot in life and I must accept it."

"I lost my husband the day yer father sent his army to attack us. Up until then, we'd been living with his threats over our heads. Every day, I worried about my husband and what would happen if the Mackenzie attacked. My worst fears came to be."

Ava sat back on her heels and sighed. "I am so very sorry."

"He was a good man, a good fighter. But yer clan sent so many warriors that it was impossible for our men to defend themselves."

At seeing the sadness in Flora's gaze, her own chest constricted. What would it feel like if Keithen was killed in battle? What if her brother attacked and, as a result, she, too, lost her husband?

"I cannot imagine."

"There is naught to be done about it," Flora said matter-of-factly. "However, I must tell ye that I do not blame ye and, despite everything, I find that I like ye."

It was hard to swallow past the lump that formed. "Thank ye for telling me this." Ava looked to Flora. "I hope we can become friends."

"We will," the woman replied. "What do ye plan to put in this garden?"

At the change of subject, Ava began to tell Flora of her plans for a healing garden.

"I MUST SPEAK to ye," Keithen said.

Ava stood and wiped dirt from the front of her skirt.

Flora excused herself and hurried indoors.

After a night's rest, he looked much better. If not for his arm in a sling, she would not know he'd been in battle. "Is something wrong?"

He nodded. "Yesterday, Ewan and I were attacked on Mackenzie lands. We'd ridden to see what was happening after seeing smoke. Yer family home was under siege."

"What did ye see? Who attacked?"

"The MacDonnell. From what we saw, the battle was hard, but neither side seemed to gain control over the other."

Her mind raced in different directions. "Can a messenger be sent to find out if my brother and mother were harmed?"

"No. Not right now. Things are too volatile. When we were caught on the lands, they accused us of being behind the attack. So now we have to wait and see what yer brother does."

"I do not know how to feel right now." Ava hung her head, overcome with the constant onslaught of bad news. It was becoming too much to bear.

Her husband's arm came around her and pulled Ava against the firmness of his chest. She wrapped her arms about his waist, not wishing to ever let go. For the first time in her life, she felt comfort and security.

The rise and fall of Keithen's breathing were like a balm to her soul, flowing and filling every part of her brokenness. The warmth of his breath on her temple soothed the fears that just moments earlier threatened to destroy her.

"Ye are not alone, Ava," Keithen said. "I will always be here for ye. Remember it. Why is yer wrist bruised?"

She leaned against his chest, embarrassed at the tears flowing freely now. It was the most perfect moment, and she wished for time to stand still so that the warmth of his embrace would never end.

"Do ye care for me?" Ava asked, needing to know.

He nodded. "Of course, I do. Ye're my wife." There was conviction in his statement, leaving no room for doubt or question. Ava's shoulders fell and lightness filled her.

"Thank ye" She looked up at him.

"No need to thank me." The corners of his lips shifted up just a bit. "Tis natural that I admit how I feel."

He looked at her again. "The bruise?"

She looked to the ground in thought. "From here, gardening, my hand slipped."

Holding her tighter, he kissed her temple. "Be with care."

It would take a long time for her to understand having a kind husband. Keithen was vastly different than any man she'd come across.

He kissed her gently, pressing his lips against hers for a lingering moment. Ava lifted to her toes and grasped his shoulders, demanding more. Keithen responded and wrapped his uninjured arm around her waist, pulling her closer as his tongue darted into her mouth.

Walking backward and falling against the wall, he trailed his lips down the side of her throat and nibbled at the sensitive skin.

Every single part of her body reacted. Shivers traveled through her limbs. It was definitely so very different with this man than with her late husband. Just a look from Keithen brought tingles of excitement.

He pulled her up against him. "I want to take ye here."

Although she was unsure how it would be accomplished, Ava nodded, eager to try.

"Pull yer skirts up," Keithen instructed. "Wrap yer legs about my waist." He fumbled with the front of his trews as he spoke.

Her breathing picked up as she peered over his shoulder, hoping no one would walk past.

"Look at me," Keithen instructed.

Ava gasped as he entered her in one swift thrust. Her body tightened in arousal and she forgot caring about anything except what happened between them.

At first, he moved slowly, pumping in a steady rhythm, filling her completely and then moving out just far enough. His breaths were hard against her throat, matching her gasps of enjoyment.

"Augh!" Keithen grunted, thrusting in harder as he neared cresting. Ava did her best to remain present in each moment, wishing to keep the beautiful memory, but her everything dissolved as she lost control and found her release. Pushing her mouth against his throat, she cried out just as his hoarse moans sounded.

For a moment, he leaned against her, pressing Ava hard against the wall. But she didn't mind, her body was too languid to feel much.

Keithen finally straightened and lowered her to the ground. "I promise to find out about yer family. It may be difficult as it is possible yer brother will declare us enemies."

"He cannot afford to attack right now, can he? Surely, many men are either injured or dead after yesterday's battle."

Her husband cupped her face, lifting it to meet his gaze. "He is a new laird and out to prove himself. Ye know him better than I do. What do ye think he will do?"

In a way, Ava felt as if she was betraying her brother. But at the same time, it could be there was a way to stop him from being foolish. "He can be impulsive at times. I do not think he is prepared for the lairdship. Father was in good health and would have lived many more years."

"All we can do is wait for now. In a few days, if we do not hear from him, it will be safe to send a messenger."

They went inside to prepare for last meal. Servants went about clearing tables and sweeping, while other people milled about waiting to eat.

A maid hurried over to her. "Milly, one of the cooks in the kitchen, cut her hand. It's bleeding horribly. Can ye come help her, Miss Ava?"

"Of course," Ava replied and looked to Keithen. "I may miss last meal."

He nodded, understanding her need to be accepted by the staff. "Aye, go."

The scene in the kitchen was chaotic. The cook was visibly upset over blood being everywhere.

The poor pale Milly whimpered as another maid clutched her cut hand. A cloth was wrapped around her hand, already turning bright red.

"Lift yer hand over yer head," Ava instructed and rushed to the fire. "I require hot water."

Pulling a piece of wood from the fire, she went to where Milly sat in the adjoining servants' dining area.

"Hold this. Continue to blow on it," Ava said to the maid who stood with Milly.

She took the maid's hand and removed the cloth. Blood spurted from the large cut that traveled from her palm straight to her wrist. Ava scooped warm water from a bowl and poured it over the injury and then pressed a clean cloth over it to dry it as much as possible.

"Take a deep breath," Ava instructed. She grabbed the hot fiery wood and pressed the reddened end to the maid's injury.

The girl screamed and the maid next to her did the same.

"What are ye doing?" The cook hurried over. Then seeing that the bleeding had stopped, the cook took the wood from Ava's hand and nodded in approval.

"Tis best to keep it covered so it does not grow infected," Ava said after wrapping the maid's hand and wrist. "I will look at it again in two days."

The maid looked away, still unhappy. "Thank ye, Mistress Ava."

It was the first time any of the servants had spoken to her by name. She hurried out of the kitchen, not wanting to linger and needing to see about Keithen.

"AVA, COME AWAY from the window. If a messenger arrives, I am sure ye will know right away," Lady Fraser said.

"It has been three days since the attack on my…er, Clan Mackenzie and still there has been no news." The tightness in her chest made it impossible to take deep breaths. No matter that Keithen had repeated that neither side had a clear victory. It didn't mean someone couldn't have made it inside and hurt her mother or brother.

The silence and lack of activity reinforced the strange feeling that something horrible had either happened or was about to.

Afternoons in the sitting room with Keithen's mother and Catriona had become her routine. They'd sip on honeyed mead and either embroidered or weaved grass baskets.

Flora had taught them to make baskets and they'd decided to make enough to decorate the tables in the great room for an upcoming visit by Laird Ross.

"When do the Ross and his family arrive?" Catriona asked in an obvious effort to distract Ava.

"Two, perhaps three days," Lady Fraser replied. "I am hopeful Esme will travel with them as well," she said, referring to her daughter who'd married a Ross.

"I hope she does as well," Catriona remarked. "I miss her terribly."

The two continued speaking about the upcoming visit while Ava fought not to jump to her feet and return to the window.

"Lady Fraser, riders have arrived at the gates." A maid walked in and looked around the room. "Laird Fraser asks that ye remain here."

At the news, all three of them rushed to the window. At the gates were a group of Mackenzie guardsmen. Two had approached the gates and dismounted. When they walked into the courtyard, they became hidden by the corner of the building.

"I am going to my bedchamber to look." Ava raced from the sitting room before anyone could stop her.

She hung over the balcony to get a good look. The men who'd arrived were familiar to her. The two had been her own father's personal guardsmen.

Closing her eyes, she did her best to hear what was being said, but it was impossible. Everyone went into the great room and out of sight and earshot.

"What can it be?" Ava asked the empty room as she paced and wrung her hands. If only she could go downstairs and ask about her family. But she dared not go against the laird's orders.

It wasn't much later that the two Mackenzie guards reappeared and, along with their contingent, rode away. Ava watched them and went to the doorway, considering if she could now go downstairs.

Keithen appeared at the top of the stairs. For a moment, his gaze met hers and then he seemed to relax.

"They came to speak to Father and ask questions regarding the attack. They refused to answer any questions about yer brother and mother when I asked. I am sorry."

Pressing her lips together in an effort not to cry, she sagged against him. "Do ye think they have perished?"

He hugged at her in return to her question. "I do not know."

"What exactly did they say?"

"Only what I said. They wished to question Father about the attack. I will know more when I go to Father's study."

As he turned, she grabbed his hand. "Please ask about my mother and brother. Also about the staff, how many were killed."

"I will."

CHAPTER THIRTEEN

LAIRD FRASER MET Keithen's gaze for a long moment. "Is what the Mackenzie accuses ye of true? That ye killed several of their guardsmen and the laird?"

It was ridiculous that anyone would fault a man for protecting his clan. "The bastards deserved death and much more for what they did to Catriona. I did not kill Laird Mackenzie. Although, he deserved it, too."

The room was silent as everyone digested Keithen's reply. Or lack thereof.

Broden met Keithen's gaze. "I am not sure Alastair Mackenzie is brave enough to declare war on us. However, I would not put it past him to send men to capture ye. I suggest ye remain in the keep for now."

"I will not hide from them," Keithen growled. "Let them bring their men and try it. What proof does he have it was me?"

"Ye have been seen on Mackenzie lands more than once. This last time when ye were with Ewan, they presumed it meant our clan was behind goading the MacDonnell to attack them," his father explained. "I do applaud the MacDonnell. He lost a lot of people when the late Laird Mackenzie attacked his villages."

"There is much to consider in all of this," Ewan Ross said

with a grin. "Rumors of masked men, invisible archers in trees. Several lairds' vengeance on the Mackenzies. I must say, I am glad I came here."

Keithen gave the man a flat look. "Ye find entertainment in strange places."

"I believe the new Laird Mackenzie is as mad as his father. We should proceed with caution," Broden interjected.

"Mad or not, if Alastair is anything like his father, he will act without care for what happens to his men," Laird Fraser replied. "I agree with Broden, Son. All of ye should remain in the keep for the time being. We will send scouts to find out what is truly happening."

The changes could actually work in his favor, Keithen considered. Although, if he ever wanted to kill the man with the birthmark, it would mean being patient. It was highly possible the bastard would be sent to hunt him down.

"Have ye seen him? This masked person?" his father asked.

Keithen shrugged. "Actually, I have. Twice. I think whoever it is has the answer to who, exactly, killed Laird Mackenzie. The man rides like the wind and is swift with sword."

"Perhaps, I should go on a hunting expedition of my own," Ewan said with a grin. "My curiosity has been piqued."

Laird Fraser shook his head. "For now, everyone must remain in the keep. Other than patrols to the nearby villages and farms to ensure all is well, the rest of guardsmen will remain here. Call those from the village," he said to Broden. "I must speak to everyone at once."

IF CLAN MACKENZIE declared war on Clan Fraser, they were evenly matched. Keithen wasn't worried about the possibility, although he did not cherish how it would affect his mother and the other women in the keep.

He walked toward the courtyard with his father, who headed to the guards' housing area. "We should send Mother, Catriona and the other women across the river to our relatives' keep."

"Not a word of this to yer mother. I will speak to her and ensure I explain it in a way that will not be upsetting. I'll suggest a trip to visit our family."

"Mother will know why ye send her away. She will fret, I am sure. But nonetheless, it would be better than her remaining here under threat of attack."

Both the Fraser and Ross guardsmen were lined up when they approached. One hundred men who would give their lives to protect their clan, heavily muscled and toned from constant sword practice, presented a formidable image.

His father straightened and silently assessed the men. "Today, we received word that the Mackenzie blames us in part for the attack by the MacDonnell." The men didn't respond and kept their gazes locked on his father.

"I will always be truthful to ye," his father continued. "I have not spoken to the MacDonnell, nor did I have anything to do with the attack, justified as it was."

The guards snickered at the truth of the last words.

When his father held his hand up, they went quiet.

"They also accuse us of killing the late laird."

At that statement, the men all looked to each other without speaking. But then, once again, they returned their attention to their laird.

"If any of ye did it, ye must inform me at once."

For a long moment, everyone waited, but none came forward. His father then paced before them, from one end of the line of men to the other.

Every so often, he stopped and spoke in low tones to several guardsmen. One man held out his hand and they shook at whatever his father had said. Keithen hoped to one day be as respected as his father was.

"I thank all of ye for yer willingness to defend our people. We have grown stronger as a clan because of it." He let out a breath. "I do know that we must remain vigilant now as the accusations can bring an attack."

When his father motioned to them, Broden and Ewan divided the guard into three groups. Broden's men would be patrolling the surrounding lands, Ewan's archers would protect from the wall and also be sent out with patrols. The third group, Keithen's men, would remain in the keep and protect it from attack.

The three leaders of the groups finished giving orders and assigning times of duty. Then, two hundred men from the village arrived.

Laird Fraser and the three men went to the gates where the information was repeated to the newly arrived warriors. They were then divided like the ones inside the keep and given their assignments. A third of the group would be camping on the lands outside the keep. Another third would camp near the village. And the final third would be inside the keep.

The entire atmosphere changed in the great room when Keithen entered. Tables were moved to one side, allowing for floor space around the hearth so people could sleep on the floor. Groups of women had arrived from the village who'd be working as cooks and assist with other chores necessary for the camps.

Keithen's mother rushed down the stairwell. "What is happening? Are we about to be attacked?"

Keithen looked over his shoulder, hoping to see his father. "No, Mother. We are preparing, just in case. But it is doubtful that anyone will attack us. No one is strong enough anymore."

There was obvious skepticism in her expression as she looked toward the doorway. "I was to go to the village today. To the market."

"Not today, Mother." Keithen took her elbow. "I can send someone to fetch whatever it is ye need."

She blew out an annoyed breath. "I will not have some man pick out ribbons and such." His mother glared at him. "Not that I will need them if we are to all die."

He almost laughed at her comment but managed a straight face. "We are not going to die."

"There ye are, I was about to come find ye." Thankfully, his father appeared in that moment. "What are yer thoughts on traveling to visit my brother across the river?" he asked his wife.

As his father painted a picture of leisurely travel to enjoy a visit, his mother's eyes narrowed. "No. I will stay here." She turned on her heel and hurried back up the steps.

"What did ye say to her?" his father asked.

Keithen shrugged. "I assured her we were not about to be attacked."

"Ye were not convincing enough."

"And obviously neither were ye," Keithen countered.

His father went up the stairs to find his wife, but Keithen knew that there would be no changing his mother's mind. She would not leave, not after what happened to her the last time she left the keep. If she feared they were to be attacked, the possibility of being captured was obviously a much more horrible possibility.

In a way, he was relieved. He did not think Catriona would be able to withstand the travel while imagining she could be taken again.

It was curious that his wife had yet to appear. He raced up the stairs to his bedchamber, which he found empty.

"Ava?" He walked into the sitting room where only Catriona and her companion remained.

"She is not here," Flora said. "She went to yer bedchamber to see what was happening. That was early this morning."

Catriona's wide eyes moved from him to the doorway. "Are we to be attacked again?"

"No, there are no warriors headed this way. No one has issued a warning. There is an untrue rumor that Father helped convince the MacDonnell to attack Clan Mackenzie." He did his best to explain what had happened. Although it was not something that would normally be told to women, he felt that Catriona had the right to know every detail.

"Father is taking precautions to keep everyone safe, although they are only threatening a few of us."

Her intelligent eye met his. "Ye and who else?"

"Broden, perhaps even Ewan."

She nodded. "Thank ye for being honest with me."

ONCE AGAIN, HE returned to the chamber he and Ava shared and looked about. Nothing seemed to be missing other than his wife. She wasn't in the kitchen, in his parents' chamber, or in the back of the keep where she'd started a garden.

As he continued to search, his concern grew. Finally, he went to the stables.

"Have ye seen my wife?" he asked one of the lads. The young man nodded.

"Aye, she left earlier today."

"Who with?"

The boy shrugged. "I do not know. I only helped her get a horse saddled."

Keithen knew exactly where his wife was headed. She was going to find out about her mother and brother.

His father would advise him to remain there and not look for her as she'd probably be safe going to her family's lands. However, with a battle just ending, there was the danger that MacDonnells continued to be hidden in the forest waiting for an opportunity to strike again.

GALLANT WAS MORE than willing to leave the confines of the corral. The horse's giant hooves pranced in place as Keithen saddled him.

Thankfully, his father was inside. Broden and Ewan busy were with their men. The guardsmen in the keep all knew their assignments and were now at sword practice, so there was little need for him to be about at the moment.

Guiding Gallant through the gates, he hesitated at noting tents being erected and a central bonfire built already. People hurried about performing all the necessary tasks to ensure everything would be set and prepared by nightfall.

His chest expanded with pride in the resilience of his clan. They worked hard to support him and his family and came together without hesitation to ensure everyone's safety.

Not wanting to attract attention, he guided Gallant to keep a slow pace until they were out of sight. Then he urged the horse to a gallop.

He rode for hours, not seeing any sign of anyone. It was strange in a way. He'd expected to have to hide from Mackenzie guards out patrolling.

It was early evening when he spotted riders and guided his horse to hide behind trees. They were Mackenzie guardsmen.

Not overly watchful, the men spoke loudly as they headed east and away from where he was. Nonetheless, he waited for a while to ensure they could not turn and see him before once again heading toward Mackenzie Keep.

Keithen was unsure what he would do once he got closer as he could not very well knock on the door and ask if his wife was there.

The forest became silent and he slowed the horse at noting the lack of sounds. Wildlife usually quieted at the presence of a horseman or other unnatural sounds.

It could be his own presence that caused it, so Keithen stopped his horse and listened intently just to be sure.

A rustling to his right caught his attention, just a second before he was tackled off the horse.

Cursing for not drawing his sword, Keithen grappled with the man. But then he was hit from behind by another man.

Keithen swung wildly and managed to punch one of them in the face. But his victory was short-lived when a third man appeared on horseback.

A hard hit to the back of his head dropped Keithen to the ground, his vision blurring. Gallant neighed and kicked in the air. Keithen pushed up from the ground to his knees and shook his head. He did his best to remain conscious. A hard kick to his side made him fall flat again.

"Tie him up," came a command.

Arms yanked back, he groaned at the pulling of the stitched-up arm. They tied his wrists together and then yanked him to his feet.

"Better keep up if ye do not wish to be dragged," the mounted man said.

He was not able to walk very long and ended up dragged twice before they gave up and threw him over the back of a horse.

Keithen threw up, his stomach heaving over and over again.

When he got loose, he would not hesitate to kill them.

"Should we take him to the laird directly?" one of the men asked.

"Why would we not?" another replied.

There was a grunt. "If he killed our laird, we should punish him a bit first. Why let the prison guards have all the fun?"

Despite finding himself beaten and bound, Keithen felt better about the situation at hearing them. Being taken to the prison guards meant he would be close to the man with the red mark.

Unfortunately, a few moments later, he was yanked from the back of the horse. They untied his hands while standing in a circle around him.

"If ye win, we will let ye go." The man who spoke was not in the least bit convincing. "Go on, hit me." He held his fists up.

Keithen knew he had no chance of beating them. However, the opportunity to get a few hits in had promise.

The first strike seemed to surprise the man as Keithen had regained some strength while riding. His fist slammed into the man's nose, sending blood spurting down his face. The man yowled and the other two laughed loudly.

"He got ye," one said as he swung and hit Keithen in the stomach.

When he bent over, another punch came to his side, followed by another. Although he'd managed a few strikes, he was no match for them.

By the time they'd grown bored with beating him, Keithen was left sprawled on the forest floor, one eye swollen shut and unable to get up.

Once again, he was tossed onto a horse just as he passed out.

AS SOON AS Keithen came to, he was aware of several broken ribs and fingers. His bound hands throbbed, and he couldn't breathe past the blockage in his nose. Blood probably.

He didn't lift his head to alert whoever was around. He was in a room, bound to a chair.

Not too far away, he heard voices of men speaking, but it was hard to hear what they said.

Someone walked up and grabbed his hair, pulling his face up. Alastair Mackenzie's face came into focus.

"I see ye decided to come to finally." The man sneered. "I apologize for the treatment upon yer capture. If it were up to me, ye would be already be dead."

Keithen coughed and winced at the pain radiating from his ribs. "Where is my wife?"

The new laird chuckled without mirth. "Do ye really expect me to believe that is the reason ye were skulking on my lands?"

"Is she here?" he managed before having to cough and spit out blood.

The man huffed. "I ask the questions here. Did ye kill my father?"

"Nay."

Alastair punched him in the stomach, and Keithen howled in pain. "Who did it then?"

He knew it didn't matter what he answered; the punishment would be the same. "I wish I knew so I could thank him."

"Ye will hang tomorrow."

Thankfully, the next hit sent him back to darkness.

CHAPTER FOURTEEN

"MOTHER!" AVA'S VOICE was hoarse from calling for her mother.

It had been sheer madness to come there.

Ava managed to make it to the keep before being caught by guards when she tried to enter through a side entrance.

Both her brother and mother were unharmed. Neither seemed particularly happy to see her.

"Why are ye truly here?" Alastair had asked repeatedly. "Did they send ye?"

"I came of my own volition. Upon hearing of the attack, I had to know ye were both unharmed."

Alastair had been drinking, his red-rimmed eyes boring into hers. "Ye lie."

Footsteps sounded, followed by her mother finally appearing, looking to her as if she was bothered. "What is it, Ava? Why are ye here?"

"Spying for them, of course," Alastair said. "She claims to be concerned about us."

"I am not lying!" Ava had dashed to her mother's side. "Now that I know ye fare well, I will return. I was worried..."

"No." Alastair motioned a guard forward. "Take my sister to

her chamber. Bind her arms and stand at the door."

Hours later, as darkness fell, she managed to slip from the bed and to her feet. However, there was nothing in the room that could be used to cut her ties. Thankfully, the guard had not had anything to tie her with and had resorted to using strips of fabric he'd torn from her underdress.

Her wrists burned from her struggles and she frantically searched the room for something to use. There was a fire in the hearth and she neared it. Then she lowered to sit on the floor and lifted her arms. Carefully and slowly, she held the bindings close to the fire.

Ava hissed as the flames scorched her skin until, finally, the fabric gave way.

She raced to the window to ascertain the possibility of escape. The chamber faced the front of the keep. The window was narrow, but she could slip out of it. Unfortunately, it was a bit of a drop to the ground below.

Just then, guards arrived at the gates, and the group called up to the gate guards who then began the process of opening them.

The small party entered the courtyard. It was then Ava noticed that a man was thrown over one of the horse's backs. Whoever it was seemed to be unconscious.

The arrivals would be the distraction she needed to get away.

She went to the bed to pull the bedding off, but then the door opened, and the guard rushed in. "What are ye doing?"

"Men arrive." She pointed to the window.

The guard gave her a narrowed look. "Get back on the bed."

Ava took a step to the bed. She was glad when the guard's curiosity got the best of him, and he went to peer out the window. She dashed to the door and raced to the end of the corridor, opposite of the way out.

There was no exit in the direction she was heading, so she knew the guard would go in the other direction, hoping to catch her.

At hearing his footsteps racing away, she dashed back into the bedchamber, closing the door behind her. She locked it and then hurried to the window.

This time, she'd have to jump without the aid of a sheet. She shimmied out feet first and then dangled from her fingertips.

When she landed on her bottom, the fall cushioned by a plush bush, Ava could have cried with gladness.

It would be a bit of a trek to get to the side entrance but, thankfully, everyone was distracted as the guards carried whoever they'd captured into the house.

Ava leaned forward to ensure the path was clear and her breath caught.

The horse the man had been brought on kicked its front hooves into the air, announcing its displeasure. The animal landed back on its legs and trotted toward her.

It was Keithen's warhorse, Gallant. Without thinking, Ava jumped onto the horse's back and kicked the animal's sides. "Go," she whispered urgently into its ears, guiding the animal straight into the courtyard.

Men scrambled out of her way as the huge beast threatened to trample them. One of the guardsmen gave her a puzzled look but then shook his head, not sure what to do.

The horse galloped at top speed out the front gates.

Ava was sure they'd be followed but, hopefully, Alastair would be too preoccupied with Keithen to care.

"Go," Ava said to the horse, digging her legs into the animal's sides. "Go!"

She had to save Keithen which meant riding to the closest Fraser allies.

Clan Ross.

HEART HAMMERING AS Gallant's huge hooves thundered across the ground, Ava could not fathom how it would be possible to save Keithen. If he wasn't already dead, then there was a chance she could arrive and ask Laird Ross to come back with her to help.

Although Laird Ross had always insisted they would be supportive, but not go to war, surely a show of force the size of Clan Ross would stop her brother from doing what he'd threatened.

She knew her husband had killed the guardsmen who'd tortured and raped poor Catriona. Ava was well aware of how he fought and his abilities. Because of it, she knew he'd not killed her father. Not because he hadn't wished to, but more because Laird Fraser would be the first accused of ordering it, being they were the clan who'd last battled against him.

The full moon hid behind clouds, making the trek toward Ross lands perilous. Never had she been more grateful for a fearless horse. Gallant seemed unaffected by the distance he ran or the fact that it was almost impossible to see.

Ava's back ached and she leaned over the horse to stretch. Unsure how much longer she had to ride, she continued in the direction of Ross lands hoping to at least run into guards on patrol or see the keep soon.

Her mind returned to the night before. How different things had been. She and Keithen had become closer. At night, they cradled against one another, the much-needed comfort she'd always craved coming from listening to his soft breathing at night and kisses every morning. Her husband was attentive when they were alone, always complimenting her and asking about any needs she had. It was strange that, in such a short time, she'd come to crave time alone with him.

And now her marriage and her husband, were slipping away.

Ava straightened, looking for any signs of buildings or people but saw nothing at that moment. Shadows confused her, but she had no doubt that she was heading in the right direction.

The beast continued forth, its strong legs crossing over the terrain until, finally, in the distance, she saw torches.

"We did it, Gallant!" Ava exclaimed, urging the horse toward the immense keep.

Upon nearing the gates, shouts sounded as men asked Ava to identify herself.

"I am Ava Fraser. I must speak to yer laird."

There was a bit of a hesitation, but then the gates opened, and she guided Gallant through. Once inside the courtyard, a guard neared. "I will see about yer horse."

Her legs were like water as she trekked up the steps to the front door. It was opened by a man who made her take a step backward.

"What is going on?" The astoundingly handsome man with his hair askew and vivid hazel eyes studied her. "Why did ye come?"

"I am Ava Fraser. My husband, Keithen Fraser, was captured by my brother. I am afraid they may hang him. I need help to save him." She did her best not to cry, but tears slipped down her cheeks. "Please. I beg ye."

Just then, two others came down the stairs. She immediately recognized the laird and his wife, Elspeth.

"Ye rode all this distance alone?" Lady Elspeth Ross studied her with admiration. "Impressive." The woman took her arm. "Ye must sit and rest."

Malcolm Ross, a commanding man who reminded her of a marble statue, looked to the man she'd been talking to. "What is happening, Kieran?"

Ava responded. "My husband, Keithen, is in trouble. He is at Mackenzie Keep. Please help me save him."

The brothers exchanged looks, communicating without words as she tried in vain to decipher the message.

"Very well." Kieran took a step toward her, his flat gaze meeting hers. "I will take men and go. But we may be too late. If yer brother seeks to hang yer husband, he may decide dawn is the perfect time."

"Or sunset," Ava said. "He may want to send for witnesses. My brother will want people to see it happen."

Although Kieran Ross was astonishingly handsome, at the same time, he was the most intimidating man she'd ever met. The man nodded. "We will find out then."

Ava hurried to Malcolm. "Thank ye. I will be forever in yer debt."

Just then, a woman burst into the room. Dressed in men's clothing, her hair pulled back, she was easy to identify. She had a remarkable resemblance to Keithen. Esme Ross' face twisted with rage.

"What did ye do?" she screamed, pointing her finger at Ava's face. The woman moved closer. "I knew this would happen. Marriage to a Mackenzie would cause Keithen's death."

Ava wasn't sure how to respond. If Keithen had come after her, then she was to blame.

"I came to get help," Ava started, but Esme cut her off with a shove.

"What ye need to do is go back to yer people. Stay there and away from my family forever," Esme cried. "Go away and never return. If my brother dies, I will hunt ye down and kill ye myself."

The woman raced from the room toward the courtyard.

"Ye should remain for the night. After the long ride, I do not think ye will be able to ride the long distance back," Elspeth said in a quiet voice. "Or perhaps ye can follow in a wagon. The horse will need to be rested as well."

"I will go," Ava said. "His horse, Gallant, cannot remain here."

Just then, a servant materialized with food and drink. Ava accepted the drink but could not fathom eating at that moment. Every moment they delayed could bring dire consequences.

"I will take it with me," she offered, and the food was quickly wrapped and packed into a sack.

Elspeth hugged her. "I wish ye well."

Refusing to meet the woman's gaze, knowing she'd lose control of her emotions, Ava rushed to catch up with the laird and his brother.

"If ye fall behind, I will not wait," Kieran warned as they walked out into the courtyard.

Ava nodded. "Please do not."

A short time later, she was astounded when they rode through the gates. Somehow, several hundred warriors had amassed and were ready to head out within the hour.

The well-armed army took her breath away and she understood why Clan Ross was feared. Every man was immobile, their expressions flat, not shifting other than when Kieran called for them to ride forward.

At the command, as one, every single horse fell into a precise fast gallop.

The thundering of hooves vibrated the ground as Ava followed in the rear with Gallant. Every sound filled her senses. The grunts of the horses, the steady beats of hooves on the ground and the whishing of the wind past her ears.

At the front, Kieran Ross rode, his shoulders back, one with the horse. She looked to the men who flanked her. "If I fall behind, do not stop, continue on. I will catch up."

The men nodded without response.

At a fast gallop, the pace was astounding. Ava knew she and Gallant would soon fall by the wayside. But she'd ride as far as possible with the Ross army.

IT WAS JUST two or three hours later that the sun rose on the horizon and they neared the edge of Mackenzie lands. It would still be several hours before they arrived at the keep, and that was if they were not intercepted by warriors.

Ava fell more and more behind. Despite his stamina, Gallant was tiring, and she finally brought him to stop. She didn't want to injure Keithen's horse.

Finally, upon arriving at a stream, she dismounted and allowed the horse to drink. "Ye must rest," she told the horse as she lowered to the water's edge and drank from the cold water.

While the horse meandered to graze, she sat at the foot of a tree, watching toward where the large Clan Ross contingent had ridden.

In her heart, she knew he still lived, but whether or not he'd be alive when Clan Ross arrived was not something Ava took for granted.

Looking up at the clouds, she prayed that they arrived in time.

Esme's words permeated her mind. Part of what she'd said was true. As much as she tried to convince herself otherwise, she was not wanted at Fraser Keep. Everyone saw her as an intruder and part of the reason so many of their people had died.

Before marrying Keithen, the plan she'd had in place had been to leave, to start a new life away from everyone she knew. Perhaps it would be best to do so at that moment. Whether Keithen lived or died was out of her hands, and if she didn't know exactly what happened, her heart would hold to the hope that he lived.

With her gone, he could go on with his life. Perhaps marry Catriona, whom he cared so much for.

Ava looked to Gallant. The horse would adapt to being hers. Perhaps he was a bit large for a woman to have but, at the same time, he was strong and would take her far.

Instead of heading to the keep, she'd go to the cottage where she'd stored items over time. It was possible to reach the small home without being seen.

No longer in a hurry to go, she nestled against the tree to sleep before heading in the new direction.

The sun was high by the time she and Gallant rode once again. Sadness settled in her chest like a boulder pressing against it, but Ava soldiered on, unwilling to look in the direction of the keep.

Her husband was possibly dead by then. If he lived, he would probably be maimed. She'd seen how horribly beaten people were by the time they were put out of their misery and hung. A cry caught in her throat and she lost control, sobbing uncontrollably. Her entire body quaked with each breath as she mourned losing the one person who'd given her a sense of security.

Keithen with his barely-there smiles and beautiful body, had, for a short time, made her feel wanted and given her a sense of belonging.

Now because of her foolish actions, he was suffering or dead and there was nothing else she could do for him.

CHAPTER FIFTEEN

THE DAMP FRIGID dungeon walls permeated through his beaten body and it relieved some of the pain. Keithen wanted to move closer to the wall, but it was impossible to gather the strength.

More surprising than the relief from the cold was that he still lived. After passing out the last time, he'd come to and found himself hanging by his arms in a room just outside the dungeon. Two men had taken turns beating him, lashing him, and finding creative ways to torture him until he could barely breathe. Just as he'd been about to lose consciousness, Keithen had been convinced he was about to die.

Waking on the dungeon floor had been surprising. Taking shallow breaths because it was impossible to breathe deeper, he lifted his head and looked around. There was no one there. The guards had been so convinced of his inability to move, they'd not bothered to close the cell door.

They were right. Even if he managed to leave the cell, the thick door out to the courtyard was closed and that would be impossible to breach.

As far as he could tell, his left leg was possibly broken and the throbbing of his right shoulder signaled it was displaced.

Whatever else was wrong, Keithen decided was not worth taking inventory.

Although there were slits that allowed for feeble amounts of sunlight in, along with a lit torch, it was impossible to tell what time of day it was. From his calculations, it had to be one day later.

Alastair Mackenzie had pronounced he'd be hung the following day, so it was to be his last day living. Keithen grunted and attempted to swallow past his parched throat. Death was not something he feared. At that point, hanging would be the least painful of what he'd gone through since being captured.

It was good that his mother and father would not be present to witness it. They probably had no idea where he was at the moment.

Had he told anyone? The stable lad would have probably been questioned. If the lad told anyone he'd gone after Ava, then perhaps Frasers would be arriving soon. He prayed his father stayed behind. As much as he wished for a familiar face upon death, he would not ever wish for his father to have to witness it.

A mouse scurried close to him, sniffed at his clothing and nibbled on the bloody edge. Keithen watched it for a long time, wondering how long the rodent had lived there. It actually surprised him that only one had appeared since he'd been there and awake. He'd thought the Mackenzie would have a dungeon full of prisoners and rodents. Instead, the dank place was riddled with spiderwebs.

They'd not bothered to put straw down for him as he was not expected to be imprisoned for long. In actuality, Keithen was more than ready for the guards to come for him. Better to know one's fate than to remain without knowing, beaten, thirsty and hungry.

He closed his eyes and imagined Ava. Just the night before, he'd held his wife and been grateful for their marriage. As much as he'd avoided feeling something for her, he'd begun to look forward to time alone with her. Like a young lad, he'd done things to get her attention. Light touches, kisses, and even volunteering to help with her dress ties.

At night, she often stayed awake longer than he did. He knew this because her movements woke him sometimes and he'd catch her looking up at the ceiling, seeming to ponder things.

"What are ye thinking of?" he'd asked her once. She'd smiled softly.

"How grateful I am to be here in this moment. Sometimes, I wish for time to stand still when we are here in bed together where it is safe."

He'd kissed her and gone back to sleep. Now, he wished he'd have stayed awake and spoken more about her thoughts and dreams. The fact he'd lost an entire year by sending her away weighed heavily on him. Although the decision had been his father's, Keithen hated to have humiliated her in such a horrible manner.

Ava was kind, caring, and beautiful and now would be widowed. If there was one reason not to die, it was that he wasn't sure what would happen to her. Hopefully, the Mackenzie would allow her to remain. If so, would he demand she marry again?

Anger surged at the thought. He would be the second husband killed by her family. Ava was treated like a pawn and now she was once again left to fend for herself.

Keithen prayed his father would offer her asylum, but he doubted it. If anything, his family would blame his death on Ava.

He allowed sleep to claim him and prayed for a quick end to the day.

FOOTSTEPS WOKE KEITHEN and he tried to sit up, but barely managed to push up from the floor. His head hung down and he took several breaths, gearing for straightening up. In his estimation, it would be easier and less painful if he was sitting and pulled to his feet than if lying flat.

Finally, he managed to sit and groaned when bolts of searing pain surged down his leg and shoulder.

"Ye look well rested," a guard said with a chuckle.

Another grunted. "Did they say to feed him?"

"No, just to get a look at him and let them know if he's living or not."

The first guard neared, and Keithen braced for what would come. The man grabbed his hair and tilted his head up. "Looks alive to me." The guard then slapped him across the face so hard, Keithen fell backward onto the ground and cried out in pain from the jostling to his leg and shoulder. "Aye, he's alive all right."

The men laughed.

"Bring him then?"

"Not yet," the first man replied, and they went to the doorway.

"He's alive and squirming," the guard informed someone outside and then settled into a conversation.

Keithen's face burned, but he barely felt it. His leg hurt worse than any of the other injuries.

It was much later that he heard voices outside. People were gathering to witness his execution. That people bothered to come was probably because they'd been promised food or something. A battle had just recently occurred. Surely, people were not interested in seeing more death.

Keithen continued listening intently for any familiar voice, but all the voices melded together.

Footsteps neared and he prepared to be jostled. Taking one last moment to pray for his soul, Keithen was more than ready to face what was to come.

"Time to be seen," one of the men said and he was pulled up to stand. Keithen groaned in pain as both his shoulder and leg hurt so horribly, he could not stop a second scream. The guards hesitated. Perhaps it wouldn't look good for the prisoner to scream louder at being moved than at the prospect of hanging.

Finally, he was half-carried, half-dragged out of the dungeon, up some steps and outside. By the time he could see the sky, he was crazed with pain, barely able to keep from blacking out.

"Do not pass out," one of the guards shouted. "We need ye aware of what is about to happen."

"I am very aware," Keithen muttered. "Will ye go on and get it over with?"

Another guard neared. "Should we tie his hands behind his back?

"He only has use of one arm," came the reply. "He can't do much with one hand to save himself. It may be more entertaining actually."

They didn't tie his hands. Instead, they half-dragged him to where a rope had been thrown over a wooden arch.

Although some people had gathered, most seemed uninterested in what was happening. They'd been ordered to be there, but Alastair could not force them to show interest. For some reason, it made Keithen feel better. Guards were lined up in a semi-circle, in case someone came and tried a last-minute rescue. He could not turn to see, but suspected archers were in place atop the gate for the same reason.

There would be no rescue. Any attempts would be impossible. He wavered when one of the guards released him and fell sideways onto the ground.

Alastair stood next to the wooden arch and looked over. "Pick him up and hold him so he does not fall," he shouted. "Do something right for a change."

Once again, he was yanked to his feet. This time, the pain was so intolerable, he became sick and vomited. Both guards released him as the spillage hit their boots and then scrambled to pick him up again.

This time, people began to laugh, and Alastair sent two other guards to take the place of the first two. Darkness edged near and Keithen could feel the pull of it. He'd not fight it. It would be better to be unconscious than to feel the squeezing of his neck.

Cold water splashed on his face and he came to. He was under the arch now and placed atop a wooden box on a newly built platform. People had quieted and, now, most looked bored.

Women tried to quiet children who'd began to complain of being hungry, while men rolled their eyes in their direction.

Finally, Alastair, who now also stood on the wooden platform, held up his hands.

"Punishment for killing a Mackenzie is death by hanging. Today, Keithen Fraser pays for killing our loyal guardsmen, by preying on them like animals."

He paused for dramatic affect. Someone coughed.

"Ye have one last chance to tell me who killed my father." Alastair neared and stared at him. "Tell me."

Keithen met the man's gaze. "Whoever killed yer father will come for ye next."

The man sneered and lifted his hand as if to hit him. But then a child began screaming and he whirled around.

"Let us get this done with. I grow bored."

The noose was slipped over his head. Keithen didn't struggle as he hoped it would be quick and over. Instead, he focused on the horizon.

There was a strange haze in the distance, like mists that came down from the mountains on some mornings.

"One moment!" A vicar rushed up the steps. "I must speak to the prisoner and see about his soul."

"There is no time," Alastair screamed. Then, upon the people murmuring about damnation, he relented. "Fine, but hurry."

The man neared. "Lower him so I can speak into his ear."

Pain tore through his entire body and he groaned at being moved, having to blow out several breaths to clear his head.

"They come. We must try to stall this," the vicar said. "Yer clan heads here."

"There is little I can do to bide time," Keithen replied, understanding why there was a haze in the horizon. "As soon as he realizes what is happening, I will be hung."

The man nodded. "Very well. Then I will have to do it."

"This man claims to be innocent," the vicar pronounced loudly. "What proof do ye have?" he asked Alastair. "I have known ye all yer life, Son. Do ye punish an innocent man?"

"Put him atop the box," Alastair ordered. Then he met the vicar's gaze. "Of course, I have proof. I have witnesses."

The people began talking to each other, asking those in the front what was happening. In the distance, riders appeared, but because of the commotion and all the talking, no one noticed.

Keithen punched the guard on his right and fell backward onto the platform. This time, people began guffawing.

Despite the pain, Keithen dragged himself over the edge, plopping to the ground below. This made people laugh even harder.

The vicar came to his side. "Very good. Perhaps pretend to pass out again."

Keithen closed his eyes as he heard the vicar being pulled away. The man protested the entire time. He wasn't sure what had happened but, once again, people began to laugh.

By the time Keithen was dragged back onto the platform and his hands tied behind his back, Alastair was livid.

Archers called down, announcing the approach of an army of warriors, which spurred the guardsmen that surrounded the people to turn and ride off.

"Hang him!" Alastair scream. "Someone get my steed."

The rope scraped his nose as it was slipped over his head. Keithen couldn't find the energy to fight any longer, although his mind scrambled for a way to keep from dying before help arrived.

Just then, arrows impaled both guards and both fell onto the platform.

Keithen turned to see Alastair's bulging eyes scanning the surroundings while the people scrambled to get away.

With a primal scream, Alastair kicked the box from under Keithen just as an arrow hit the laird on the side.

At first, Keithen didn't feel anything. His body was so wracked with pain that he did not sense the danger of imminent death.

But then the realization that he could not breathe broke

through.

Within moments, he would die.

Despite the tightening of the noose, Keithen fought to breathe, his body convulsing. As much as he told himself to let go and allow the inevitable, the instinct to live was strong.

A primal scream permeated through the fog of his struggles and then he fell to the platform, gasping for breath.

Someone had cut him down. There was no one that he could see but gasping for breath took precedence over anything else.

Through sheer will, Keithen managed to maneuver himself to the edge of the platform and roll to the ground below. The impact knocked what little bit of breath he had from his lungs.

The clash of swords rang through the air.

People screamed, scampering in all directions. To avoid being trampled, he rolled under the protection of the platform.

Pain shot through him from his broken leg. His shoulder had somehow moved back into place, probably from one of the falls.

Keithen closed his eyes and listened to the sounds of rescue and then all went dark.

"IT WILL BE a long time before ye can get about without pain," the healer informed Keithen several days later. He'd finally managed to remain awake long enough to know he was back at Fraser Keep in his own bedchamber.

Because of his broken leg and other injuries, it was impossible to move without excruciating pain. Even now, he wondered if he'd live past all the damage that had been done. Instinctively, he knew his worst injuries were not visible. The pangs that ran down his back from being kicked signaled all was not well.

"Where is my wife?" he asked. "Did she remain at Mackenzie Keep?"

Esme, his sister, huffed. "In all probability. That is where she belongs." She neared the bed and pressed a hand to his cheek. "What ye need to concern yerself with is healing. I will be here to ensure ye do." She smiled down at him. "I love ye, dear brother."

Never had he been more grateful for his sister's unnaturally accurate archery skills. From atop a moving horse, Esme had struck the rope and saved his life.

"Ye are an amazing archer," he said, slurring the words as a result of whatever was in the tonic the healer had given him.

His sister shrugged. "I was not about to lose ye."

"What happened? Who came with ye to save me?"

She lowered to a chair. "Two hundred Ross warriors and all of Clan Fraser. The Mackenzie surrendered without much of a fight. Malcolm is meeting with the other Laird Mackenzie to decide what is to be done. Malcolm knows Clan Ross cannot take over the lands without threat from other larger Mackenzie clans."

"Alastair lives then?"

Esme's face shuttered. "I believe so."

"Ye shot him, didn't ye?" Keithen met her gaze. "Why didn't ye kill him?"

His sister gave a one-shouldered shrug. "My husband would be cross if I started a war."

Keithen shook his head. "Where did ye shoot him?"

"Between the legs."

Despite hating the man, Keithen couldn't help but shudder. "Well, that was not what I expected to hear. Do not ever tell Ava this."

His sister hesitated and finally nodded. "If she returns, I will not speak of it."

Broden walked into the room, his gaze boring into Keithen's. "No one has seen her since she fell behind when following the men from Ross Keep."

He fought against the lure of sleep. "Ye must find her. She did not return to Mackenzie Keep. I am sure of it."

"Scouts have been sent. Yer wife will be found." Broden studied him for a bit. "Why were ye on Mackenzie lands?"

Keithen didn't want to admit that he'd gone after Ava. But being that she was gone as well, he was sure they'd figure it out. "Ava went to find out if her brother and mother had been killed in the MacDonnell attack. I went after her."

"I knew she was the cause of this," Esme snapped. "Ye should have let her go. If she does not wish to return, then so be it."

He'd not stopped asking himself why Ava had not appeared yet. He suspected it could be guilt over what had happened to him. After learning she'd ridden so far alone in the night to rally Clan Ross, he'd been both impressed and shocked at her actions.

However, now she'd yet to appear and from all accounts, she had Gallant with her.

"Esme?" he started and his sister arched a brow. "Did ye speak to her?"

His sister nodded. "Aye, I did. I told her she was the reason for the situation and if ye died, I would find her and kill her myself."

Keithen closed his eyes. "Let me know as soon as she is found."

"I will take the patrol on a wider circle." His friend's assurance brought only a bit of confidence that Ava would be returned to him.

Just then, another set of footsteps sounded, but Keithen could not force his eyelids to open.

"Keithen's horse has returned," someone said.

CHAPTER SIXTEEN

FOR TWO LONG days, she'd been in the dark crate that rocked side to side on the back of a wagon.

Ava had given up on crying or attempting to scream past the dirty rag that had been stuffed in her mouth. The cramped space stunk from her own urine and lack of ventilation, and she pressed her face against the side, attempting to get fresh air and to see through the tiny cracks between jagged boards.

Sea air permeated the crate and she knew that, soon, she'd be loaded aboard a ship and taken far away.

When a man neared the wagon, she kicked the crate. He looked in her direction for only an instant, shrugged and then kept walking.

Frustrated that every effort had failed, she fell back against the other side of the crate and tried to think of what to do.

If only she'd stayed at the small village she'd come upon after being left behind. The small village of Kildonan was not far from Ross lands, so she'd decided it was best to continue south. The following night, a pair of men accosted her while she'd slept.

She'd expected to be attacked by them after being tied up, but when they'd lifted her skirts and seen blood, they pronounced her to be unclean. If not for the circumstances, she would have laughed at the thought that men who considered raping a woman would then call the woman dirty.

"Mayhap we can keep her healthy long enough to sell her," the man with appalling teeth had muttered.

They'd bound and gagged her and thrown her over a horse, and finally put her into a wooden crate. She'd struggled and not made it easy for them to stuff her into the tight space, but they'd overcome her easily.

Once again, her stomach cramped, and she hoped not to have to relieve herself. Silently, she prayed to be let out of the crate.

Moments later, the cramping became worse and she doubled over, moaning. Wave after wave of pain tightened her midsection unlike anything she'd felt before. It was too dark to see, but the smell was unmistakable.

Blood.

She wasn't sure how long it continued until, finally, she fell into a fitful sleep.

Light followed by fresh air made Ava wake.

A man's face came into focus.

"She's gotten worse. No one will give us any coin for her. She won't finish the trip. She'll be dead in a day or two."

Two other faces peered down at her. The men who'd taken her. One of them wrinkled his nose. "Why is she all bloody?"

"Leave her. She'll die soon," the first man assured them. They replaced the top on the crate.

Moments later, the crate was lifted and lowered to the ground. Then not so gently, it was shoved against something.

The putrid smell of rotting fish made Ava nauseous and she heaved, praying not to get sick since the rag was still shoved into her mouth.

Lifting to her knees, she pushed at the top of the crate with her head, and it gave way. The men had been so convinced of her imminent death that they'd not bothered to nail it shut.

"Ye're a bloody mess." A craggy face appeared over her. It was hard to tell if it was a man or a woman who stood next to the crate. "Here." The person held out a dirty hand. "Come on, I'll help ye out."

Ava did her best to stand, but her legs wobbled. She fell against the side of the crate and it tipped over. She grimaced when her shoulder hit the ground but was so happy to be out of the crate, it didn't matter if it hurt.

"Ah, ye're tied up," the person said, yanking the cloth from her mouth. "Let's see here."

She now guessed the person was a woman because she wore long, dirty, gray skirts. "I normally do not help strangers, but ye are left behind, so I am thinking no one's coming for ye."

"Water?" Ava croaked.

"None to be had," the woman said, cackling and untying her hands. "Got a bit of ale." She held up a bottle with a cracked top. "Only a sip."

Her arms refused to move, so she tipped her face up and the woman pressed the bottle to her lips. The ale was bitter, but she welcomed the wetness of it.

"Thank ye," Ava finally said. She remained sitting on the ground, her blood and urine-stained skirts collecting dirt.

"Ye should go over and wash up." The woman motioned to the water's edge with her head. "Salt water will help with the healing"

Ava wasn't sure about the healing properties, but she did have to wash up. Although she would have preferred an alternative to salty water, it was better than nothing.

"Where am I? What place is this?"

"Shandwick," the woman replied, walking away. "Ye be with care. Many men look for young lasses for the taverns or to sell to traders." She pointed to a ship that had drifted away from the shore. "Ye were probably meant for that one." The woman continued rambling as she walked away.

Once Ava got to her feet, painful tingles traveled down her arms. But at least feeling was returning.

On wobbly legs, she managed to make it to the water's edge

and walked into the water until it reached her knees.

The water was frigid but, for some reason, it felt exhilarating. Being in the water, washing away days of filth meant she was free.

Having to wash away all the blood, she continued forth until she was waist deep and then began splashing water to her arms and face. She ensured to wash between her legs and then rubbed the fabric of the skirts in an effort to get as much excrement from them as possible.

Shivering, she hurried from the water. Soaked from the waist down meant she'd be very cold if her skirts did not dry by sundown.

Like every other port village, it was untidy and probably dangerous for a woman alone. She blew out a breath as she tried to figure out what to do.

Finally, she walked in the direction the old woman had gone. After a few minutes, the woman came into view as she tottered into a tiny, lopsided house. Ava hurried to the door and knocked.

"Ah, it's ye," the woman said, not seeming surprised. "I suppose ye may as well come in. Tis not a good place for ye to be out and about." The woman's keen gaze took her in. "Have ye any coin?"

The question surprised her. Ava did keep a small sack of coins in the pocket hidden in her skirts. But she wasn't about to admit it to a stranger.

"Nay. I was robbed of everything when I was attacked. My family will pay a ransom for me," she added, not sure which family she referred to.

One way or another, she had to get away from there. "Is there someone who could take me home?"

The woman shrugged and lowered to a stool. "I do not have a horse. Thomas may take ye, but I've not seen him in days."

"I promise to send ye payment and…" Ava looked around the shabby surroundings. "Fabric for a new dress if ye help me."

The woman brightened. "I do need a new dress." She got to

her feet with surprising spryness. "Come along then."

They traversed one of the most interesting and, at the same time, terrifying places Ava had ever been. Men called out as they walked by asking the old woman how much for Ava. She hunched her shoulders, allowing her hair to fall and hide her face, but it did not stop her from attracting attention.

Although not as painful, the cramping in her abdomen continued. It was obvious that she was suffering from more than her monthly courses. At the moment, however, she refused to think about what was actually occurring.

The woman stopped at a shack and rapped on the door. "Thomas."

An instant later, the door opened, and a man emerged. With hair past his wide shoulders and a full beard, it was impossible to describe his features. He grunted at the old woman. "What do ye want today, Hilda?"

"This woman claims her family will pay a ransom for her. I want a portion of what they pay."

His icy gaze moved to Ava. Something flickered a sort of softening, but it was gone when he shook his head. "No, I do not trust ye."

Not sure if he spoke to her or the woman, Hilda, Ava waited.

"There won't be another ship for days. Ye have time."

He looked to Ava again. "Where are ye from?"

She considered the closest clan but discarded returning to Clan Ross. "Clan Fraser near Munlochy."

"Ye can get there sooner if ye take a birlinn and cross by water," the old woman suggested, obviously eager for the fabric Ava had promised.

"I will ensure ye are paid for it." Ava considered the amount she had with her, along with what she kept in the bedchamber at Fraser Keep. It would more than pay for the man's help.

She clutched at her stomach when pain struck again. "I need to sit." Stumbling to a stool outside the man's door, she lowered to it and wrapped her arms around her lower midriff.

"She's lost a bairn. There's nothing much to worry about other than the woman will be in pain for a few days."

At the woman's words, Ava squeezed her eyes shut and blew out a breath. She'd not been aware of being with child until the last night she was alone in the forest when the first pangs had begun. It had been over two months since her last courses. The hard riding had been what killed her unborn child.

So much had occurred because she'd been rebellious and disobeyed Keithen. Neither her brother nor mother had been harmed in the battle. Additionally, neither had cared one bit that she'd come to ensure that they were well.

Instead, Alastair had accused her of being part of the reason for the attack, even insinuating she helped plan it.

Although her mother had not been overly welcoming, she'd acted as if it were a bother that Ava was there.

Tears burned her eyes, but she refused to allow them to fall. Why did she keep trying to gain her family's care? They would never change.

"When can we leave?" Opening her eyes, she looked up into the man's grayish ones.

After looking up to the sky, he then turned away from the docks. "In the morning. Ye can stay here if ye wish." He motioned to the shack. "Up to ye."

Ava looked to the older woman, but she shook her head. "I do not have room for ye."

For the rest of the evening, Ava sat on the stool or paced outside Thomas' shack. The cooling salty air made her shiver since her clothes remained wet. Then to make matters worse, the salt on her skin was itchy. Never had she been so miserable. Ava returned to the stool, crossing her arms in an effort to maintain warmth. Only when it was absolutely inevitable would she go into the man's shack.

Moments later, Thomas appeared from wherever he'd gone. He carried a bucket, which he placed next to her.

The smell of food made her mouth water, but she didn't dare

touch the bucket. He ducked into the shack and brought out another stool and lowered to sit on it. Then digging into the bucket, he brought out a loaf of bread that he tore in two, followed by a bowl that spilled over with a sort of stew. "They only had one bowl left, so we'll have to share," he explained.

Ava didn't care. She dipped a piece of bread into the stew and carefully scooped up some of the contents.

They ate in silence. The man made no attempt at conversation. Ava was just as comfortable without it.

When they finished, he offered her a drink from a wineskin, and she took it. After she took a drink, she shoved her hand into her skirts and pulled out a silver coin and held it out. "Thank ye."

With a nod, he took the coin. The sum would have more than paid for the food. Ava hoped that it gave him more confidence in agreeing to take her back.

He stood. "I am going to return this. Ye can come along if ye wish or ye can go inside. There is fresh water for ye to wash up with."

Rinsing away the salty water sounded good, but Ava wasn't sure she could walk as far as she'd seen him go. "I am afraid that I cannot go very far. I am still in pain."

He nodded and walked away.

Inside the shack, it was cleaner than the old woman's. The few belongings the man had were placed on a shelf next to a small cot. The only other furnishings were a table and a trunk. Both were well made and clean.

She noted he kept two buckets of water and a small tub that could be used for washing clothes or bathing. It was interesting that someone who lived on the docks where danger lurked and everyone was out to make coins would live so sensibly.

When he returned and ducked through the doorway, the already too small space shrank.

"I brought more fresh water for ye and this," he said as he held out a faded frock. "I will be outside."

Ava wasn't sure what to think. How could a virtual stranger

be so kind? She was sure he was not what he seemed. Or perhaps he was what he seemed: a miscreant, someone who took women and sold them off to the highest bidder.

How far could she get if she slipped away and headed south? There was a loch between Ross and Fraser lands that had to be traveled over or around.

With no horse and a lack of clear direction, returning home seemed impossible.

Finally, she gave in and quickly undressed to her chemise. With quick movements, she washed her body, hating that the water turned bloody from the dried blood between her legs. She pulled the faded frock on over her head and then proceeded to tear her chemise into strips. From the strips, she fashioned a strap around her waist, she then took two strips and tied them to the front, between her legs and then to the back. She fashioned a wrapped bundle that would hopefully absorb any further bleeding to the strap between her legs. Once that was accomplished, she felt relieved to not be bleeding on her clothing.

She walked out and tossed the dirty water. Thomas sat on a stool with a piece of wood in one hand a knife in the other. He slid the blade deftly through the wood. "Sleep well, lady. We will head out early."

Ava nodded. "Where should I sleep?"

He looked at her. "The cot. I will sleep on the floor."

Clean and with food in her stomach, Ava lay on the cot, grateful for not being still locked in a crate.

If only she'd not gone to see her family, things would be so different in that moment. But she'd been so stubborn and had a habit of going into things without thinking it through.

She let out a sigh and prayed that Keithen was alive and well. Then, when the door opened, she prayed that the man, Thomas, would not harm her, but instead help her get home.

To her surprise, he didn't even look in her direction. He instantly doused the lantern on the small table and then spread a blanket he pulled from the trunk onto the floor.

Within moments, his soft snores sounded, and Ava, too, fell into a slumber.

"WE WILL LEAVE shortly. I will go pull my birlinn. Ye can come after breaking yer fast."

Ava sat up and rubbed her eyes. Her fast? She hurried to find a bucket to relieve herself and then once that was done, rinsed her face and hands.

On the table was a bowl with what looked to be mutton and bread. Ava ate the portion he'd left for her and then dutifully rinsed out the bowl.

She would make sure the man was paid well for everything he'd done for her. Hopefully, he did not have sinister plans in mind and would indeed ensure she arrived back at Clan Fraser in less than three days.

Moments later, she and two men who'd been recruited to help with the rowing were on a birlinn crossing a span of water. It was the first time she'd been on a vessel like the one Thomas owned. He seemed at ease on the water, maneuvering it to the opposite shore by allowing the sea to set the speed.

When they came to the opposite shore, several men hurried out the help pull the birlinn to the beach. They all spoke in fast tones, seeming to be catching up on latest events.

The talking and laughter brought to mind the men at Fraser Keep, who often remained after practice to stand around and talk of home and families. For the first time, she'd finally felt at home, somewhat belonging. However, Esme had reminded her she was truly not wanted or needed there.

If she did return to Fraser Keep, perhaps it would be best to ask Keithen to allow her to go into a nunnery. The family would no doubt urge him to do so. After everything that happened, how could they not wish her gone?

THE NEXT DAY, she spotted a village in the distance. Ava recognized it. The coin purse was not heavy, but she had more than enough to pay the man who'd helped her. He'd been respectful and silent most of the trip. Although curious about him, Ava didn't pry and ask any questions. Whatever his reason was for living the way he did was his own.

"I've changed my mind," Ava told him as he guided the wagon he'd borrowed from acquaintances once they'd landed on the opposite shore. "Just take me to that village."

Without even a shrug, he guided the horses in the new direction. Slipping her hand into her pocket, she untied her coin bag.

Drizzle began to fall, and Ava hunched against it. She'd no cloak, no shoes and only the worn frock the man had found for her. A man who stood under an overhang by the tart shop watched them with curiosity, but then disappeared through a door.

She looked about hoping to see a familiar face, but the only other person was a young man pulling two goats.

"Here." Ava held out her coin bag. "I hope it is enough for yer troubles. Thank ye so very much."

The man took the coin bag, plucked out three coins and handed it back to her. "Get yerself a cloak and shoes."

Moments later, she entered the tart shop and the woman behind the counter gasped. "Lord above, what happened to ye?"

CHAPTER SEVENTEEN

CATRIONA MCKAY HELD her face up to the cloudy sky and closed her eyes. After being indoors for over a year, she now relished time outdoors. Although she'd yet to go further than the keep grounds, it was progress from the confines of the house.

Nightmares continued to bring back images of the days she'd been brutally attacked at the hands of Mackenzie guardsmen. At least they didn't come nightly any longer. However, they happened often enough that she could not stop the terror that seized her at being approached by men.

It was only recently that she could spend time in the great room. But she always sat at a table in the corner, with only Flora, her companion, and whatever other women decided to join them.

"There ye are," Esme walked toward her. "I wondered where ye had gone off to."

Her childhood friend's assessing look came next. "Ye look good. Ye have gained back some weight."

Catriona couldn't help but smile at Esme's motherly actions when she touched her face and met her gaze. "How do ye feel today?"

"I am not sick," Catriona said. "I am well and have taken over working in the gardens. Today with the drizzle, the plants will be happy."

"Aye," Esme let out a breath. "It is quite a dreary day."

"When do ye go back?" Catriona reached for Esme's hand. "I hate it when ye leave."

"Not for a while. I will not leave until I am absolutely convinced Keithen will be well." Her friend looked up at the second story windows. "He is not well at all right now."

Catriona had loved Keithen Fraser most of her life and the thought of any future without him made her ache physically.

"I am sure he will recover. He is strong," she said, trying to convince herself as well as Esme. "Ye will see."

"Have ye gone to see him?"

Ever since Keithen married Ava Mackenzie, Catriona had done her best to keep her distance. As much as she treasured her friendships with Esme and her brother, he was not to be hers, ever. And although she accepted it, it still hurt.

"Nay, but I will. How is he faring?"

Esme shook her head. "So many injuries." A tear trickled down her face and Esme wiped it away. "A broken leg, bruising everywhere, his face so swollen it is hard to tell if it's really him. Thankfully, he spends most of the day sleeping."

A shudder traveled through Catriona. Had everyone said the same about her when she'd returned from being subjected to days of men taking turns with her? Most of them were violent, enjoying hurting her.

Esme, ever perceptive, touched Catriona's shoulder. "We should go inside. The rain is getting harder."

THERE WERE A few people keeping dry in the great room. A group of men sat at a table, talking. At another table, Catriona presumed the men's wives rocked young babes as they waited out the rain before heading home. By the fireplace, two guards stood. One of them was Broden, whom she'd known for many years. The other was Ewan Ross, the man who'd come there to provide help to the clan.

"Esme," Catriona said. "Are the Ross guards to remain here?"

Since the late Mackenzie's death, the threat was considerably lower so she'd hoped most of the new strange men would leave.

Her friend shrugged. "Father says they will. Especially as there are reports the new laird may be very sick and could possibly be removed from leadership."

"Good. I hope the Mackenzie Clan is disbanded," Catriona said with a snarl. "I hate them."

"I hate them as well," Esme said.

Catriona frowned, considering Ava Fraser. "Except for Ava. She is kind."

Esme huffed. "She is the reason for Keithen almost dying. She is an idiot."

It was best not to argue with Esme. Once her friend made up her mind about something, it was impossible to change it. Although Catriona understood why Ava did what she'd done, it had been reckless.

"If it was Fraser Keep that had been attacked, would ye not wish to know if yer mother and brother survived?"

Narrowing her eyes, Esme considered her words. "I would find out in a way that would not get my husband killed."

"May I have a word?" Broden pulled Esme aside.

Just as Catriona was about to turn away, Ewan Fraser neared. "Miss Catriona, it is good to see ye out."

Her heart thudded. She'd yet to have a conversation with a man other than the laird and Keithen. "I-I, aye."

Hazel eyes met hers for a second before she looked away. "Is there a seamstress at the village? I require new tunics. The three I brought with me are either torn through or ripped."

Unsure what to do, she panicked. "I will mend them. Just bring them to me at last meal."

"Ye do not have to do it."

"Bring them I said," she snapped and hurried away.

KEITHEN TESTED HIS ability to sit up by himself. Pain from the tension around his midsection made it difficult, but he managed it. His eyes felt hot, so he knew a fever was present, but it was normal. After all, his body was fighting to heal. Working his tongue around his mouth, he was surprised to find only one spot on the right side where a tooth was missing. He'd done the best he could to keep kicks from his face but had failed a couple of times.

He had to speak to his father and ensure someone was sent to find out where Ava was. Unable to stand on his leg, he could not hope to walk out of the room. "Guard!"

No one entered and he huffed in annoyance. Hopefully, a maid would appear soon, and he could send for his father.

All day, it had rained, and he wondered if Ava had found shelter from it. If she had remained at Mackenzie Keep, he wasn't sure if he could accept it.

On one hand, she'd saved his life by riding to the Ross Keep to get help. But on the other hand, why had she abandoned Gallant? The horse had returned unharmed and saddled.

If she'd been accosted, surely they'd have kept the warhorse as it was an astonishingly beautiful horse.

Keithen grunted as pain gripped him. Then again, Gallant was not tame enough to allow just anyone near him.

Finally, the door opened and Broden entered. "Ye bellowed?" His friend lowered to a chair and proceeded to bite the side of his thumb nail.

"I thought ye were out on patrol," Keithen said. "Why did ye return already?"

"No news. No one has seen or heard of a lass matching Ava's description riding about."

Keithen gave him a droll look. "She would not be riding since the horse returned."

"How do ye know? What if she returned to Mackenzie Keep and retrieved a horse there? We do not know where Gallant was released from."

It was true. However, his gut told him something had happened to Ava.

"If yer wife wished to return, she would have arrived by now." Broden gave him a pointed look. "I think she is at Mackenzie Keep. It is impossible to breach Mackenzie Keep as the gates are closed and heavily guarded."

"What should I do?" Keithen asked, knowing Broden did not have a reply.

His friend shook his head. "All ye can do is wait and recover. Right now, there isn't much that can be done."

Just then, his father and mother entered. His mother carried a tray with a bowl of soup and bread. "Good evening, Son," she greeted with a smile. "It is good to see ye sitting up."

She looked to Broden. "Help him to straighten, please, dear."

Doing his best to keep from grimacing at being pulled up and pillows pushed behind his back, Keithen then waited for his mother to place the tray over his lap.

"Now," she pronounced. "Yer father and I will keep ye company while ye eat."

Broden met his gaze for a moment. "I will see about last meal then." He left the room and both his parents looked to him with expectation.

"Eat," his mother instructed.

"Father, I must insist that scouts be sent to find out if Ava is safe. She saved my life and I am concerned that no one has seen her."

His father nodded. "In all probability, the lass is scared to return. After all, she is the cause of what happened to ye. Several of our men have been seriously hurt, one is near death from the clash with the Mackenzie guards. All because of her impulsive notion to go to our enemy's keep."

"I like the lass, but I do not care for a wife who is disobedient," his mother said with a frown.

"Do ye not think, in a similar situation, Esme would have done the same?" he asked, looking first to his father and then to his mother. "I am willing to wager she would have been here without hesitation."

"Be that as it may," his father said. "I am reluctant to send men into dangerous territory. I prefer to wait and see if news comes."

There was little he could do. It would be months before he could ride, much less fight. Keithen peered down at the soup. "I only ask that men be sent to surrounding villages on the road from Clan Ross to here to ask about her."

His father let out a sigh. "Very well. They will be dispatched tomorrow."

"Eat," his mother urged. "Yer soup will get cold."

While he ate, his mother spoke of inconsequential things, mainly about staff in the keep and visitors who'd overstayed their welcome. Her anecdotes were just what Keithen needed at the moment. He and the laird had always enjoyed her descriptions and animated imitations of the villagers who'd been there for hearings.

Once her parents left, a couple of men came to help him prepare for the night. By the time the healer's awful tincture flowed down his throat, he was so tired that he would have easily fallen asleep without it.

CHAPTER EIGHTEEN

AVA THANKED THE peddler who brought her to Mackenzie Keep. The man was setting up to sell his wares just outside the walls. Immediately, people emerged and began to bargain. She hurried through the gates and inside. The sooner she could retrieve some belongings and, hopefully, some coins from her mother, the sooner she'd leave forever.

Her mother was nowhere to be found. In the great room, only a few servants milled about. As per usual, no one felt comfortable enough to remain in there.

"Where are my brother and mother?" she asked a young woman, who started at seeing her. "Mistress Ava. I-in yer brother's chambers."

She hurried up the steps, stopping only upon seeing two guardsmen standing outside the door. Both gave her a quick once over and said nothing.

News that she was the one to inform the Ross about Keithen's capture must not have reached them because they allowed her to pass without speaking.

The stench in the room was horrible. It was almost as if someone had already died. But instead, she found Alastair seated on a chair, drinking.

"Ah, there she is. My sister appears to ensure I die." Alastair's words slurred. "What do ye want?"

The healer who had a cloth tied around his face to cover his nose and mouth hurried to her. "He will not allow me to clean his wound. It has festered." Thankfully, the man handed her a cloth and she tied it around her face.

"Where is Mother?"

When Alastair ignored the question, the healer replied, "She's gone to yer uncle's keep in the north."

"She left ye?" Ava neared her brother. "Ye cannot be left alone right now."

When Alastair threw his head back and laughed, she quickly sprinkled herbs into his ale and motioned a servant closer.

The green-faced young maid, who looked like she was about to get sick, managed to pour more ale into the cup and Ava noted the healer added more herbs when Alastair looked to Ava.

"I would have left if I were her. When I die, all of this goes to no one." He motioned with one hand.

"Ye do not have to die. Allow me to help," Ava told him in a flat tone. She went to the window to get fresh air. But it did little to help.

"Guards!" she called out when Alastair slumped forward moments later.

The men were reluctant to enter, but finally did. They lay her brother atop the bed and then hurried back out.

Ava then looked to the maid. "Go instruct the cook to boil water. Bring back cold water for now."

Along with the healer, she was able to peel away the bloodied cloths from between her brother's legs. The arrows had pierced his manhood and his lower abdomen. The lower injury had caused enough damage that he would never perform as a man again.

"The rotting flesh will all have to be cut away. But even then, the festering has spread."

"Why did ye not give him herbs before this?" Ava demanded.

"Ye could have had guards subdue him and…"

"I tried, but the guards would not listen to me."

Ava understood. Alastair and her father ruled through fear. Punishments for disobedience had always been horrible.

Ava went to the doorway.

Two guards looked at her. "Ye should go, ensure the keep is secure. I am not sure my brother will live much longer. The clan will be vulnerable."

Ava's gut tightened. In truth, her brother would, in all probability, succumb to his wounds. The injury was horribly infected. Nonetheless, she had to try to save him.

It took them several hours to get the infected area cleansed, and most of the infected flesh cut away. Ava stood by as the healer placed leeches into the wound. The small creatures would hopefully eat enough of the remaining infected area to save him.

Alastair was unconscious, his pale face wet with perspiration. Ava pushed hair from his brow. Her heart was breaking for the man who'd either die or survive as a maimed man. All for what?

"He has another injury to his side," the healer pointed out.

Ava studied her brother as they did what they could for the green, infected wound.

By ruling over people without care for their welfare, their father had left her brother with nothing.

In his quest for power, he'd acquired allies through force and threats of war. Understandably, none of them were truly loyal to them and had cut ties as soon as he'd died. When everyone broke ties at once, it proved impossible to bring them back.

After all the damage her father had done, it was only fitting that, now, his family had to pay the price. However, seeing everything crumble and her brother on his deathbed remained one of the most horrible experiences of her life.

Needing to get something to eat, Ava went downstairs. She looked around the empty, dim great room and immediately compared it to the Fraser's. There, people mingled, came to have their grievances heard and then remained for last meal.

The people of Clan Fraser actually cared for their laird and his family. Together, they shared life moments and celebrated.

Here, no one would come to inquire about Alastair's health. It was rare that anyone outside the family felt comfortable enough to remain for a meal. It was so sad that her parents had preferred this type of austere life.

When she returned to her brother's bedchamber, the linens on the bed had been changed and, already, the room smelled better.

Her brother continued to sleep. Ava wasn't sure what Alastair would do upon waking. She hoped he would be too ill to do anything harmful, but one never knew with her brash brother.

"Go get something to eat and rest," Ava told the healer. "I will remain here with him."

She went to the window and peered out at the night sky.

How was her husband? If she were there, she'd be caring for him. But in all probability, they'd not allow her near him.

Somehow, she would get word to him that she was well and would be going to live with her mother at her uncle's keep.

Even if Alastair recovered, he would not want her there. She turned to the bed and found that her brother was awake and watching her.

"I do not wish to live."

His words were clear. Ava hurried to the bedside and lowered to sit.

"Ye are Laird Mackenzie. Ye must live to ensure the people are taken care of. Who will be laird if ye die?"

He turned away from her. "I do not care. Why should I?"

"A laird puts his people first. That is what a true laird does. Ye have an opportunity to change, Brother. To do well."

"I can feel it." Alastair closed his eyes. "Death is closing in on me. What will ye do?"

Ava took his hand. "I will remain here with ye, if ye need me."

Turning to her, his half-closed eyes met hers. Alastair was so very pale, with dark circles under his eyes and his lips were a purplish-blue. "Remain with me."

Her brother closed his eyes and, moments later, his hand went limp. Ava's eyes rounded.

"Alastair?" She hovered over him. "Alastair!"

THE HEALER WALKED in the next morning and glanced to Ava. "Is he?"

"Aye, he died last night. We must not tell anyone."

The healer nodded and went to the window. The room still reeked of infection, making it impossible to breathe properly. Ava herself had slept next to the window.

"If word gets out that yer brother is dead, I am positive we will be attacked immediately."

Ava shrugged. "I am not sure about it. No clan wishes to garner my uncle's ire. Although he's not as impulsive as my father, he is very powerful."

Moments later, there was a knock, and Ava slipped out, not allowing the young man to look in. "Ye must deliver a message to my uncle immediately. Alastair needs his assistance."

The man nodded. "Of course, Mistress Mackenzie."

She didn't bother correcting him that her name was now Fraser.

"Ride without stopping," she instructed. "Take the swiftest horse."

When she walked back inside, the healer turned to her. "I am hopeful they will arrive within two days. We cannot possibly maintain the illusion that yer brother lives."

"We have no choice," Ava said wearily. She'd not slept for two days other than dozing for a few moments on the chair. "We will take turns staying here. I will instruct the servants that my brother does not wish to be disturbed."

"Who do ye think will take over this clan?"

Ava pictured her uncle's family. "I do not know. He has three sons. So perhaps the second born, Cayden, since the oldest cousin, the first born, will take over for my uncle when he dies."

FOR THE NEXT two days, Ava and the healer managed to keep everyone at bay. Being her brother was not well-liked, no one had insisted to enter the room. The only person who seemed suspicious was the leader of the guard, who insisted her brother would want to hear his reports.

Ava crossed her arms and stared up at the warrior whose broad shoulders prevented her from seeing around him. "My brother is very sick. I doubt he will remember anything ye tell him. The healer and I are doing our best to maintain Alastair's dignity," Ava whispered. "He was shot between the legs, as ye know."

The man grimaced and nodded. "Alastair does not wish anyone to see the extent of his injuries, which cannot be covered because…well, there are leeches being used."

This time the warrior paled. "Leeches?"

Ava nodded. "Which is why I doubt he will be able to focus on a word ye say." She reached for his forearm. "Please do not say a word. He will be most cross at me for saying what I have."

After a moment, the man sighed. "Very well. I am sure ye will send word when I can speak to him."

"Err.. aye, of course. I must inform ye that the Mackenzie of the north will be arriving in a day or two."

"Very well." The man turned and walked away.

Ava let out a long breath. Would her life ever be normal? Would she ever have a day without a life hanging in the balance or without fear of what will happen next?

The next day slogged by until, finally, late in the day, a small army appeared on the horizon.

Ava prayed they were Mackenzies.

Another attack would too much to bear at the moment.

Last meal was presided over by her uncle, the Mackenzie. He was a calculating man who, like her late father, measured his gain before making decisions. Unexpectedly, it was decided that another relative, Atholl Mackenzie, a cousin, would be given the lairdship of her clan. Ava suspected it was either because the man was spineless or because her uncle was indebted to him.

To her, it didn't matter. Other than needing a place to live, Ava wanted nothing to do with her family.

Her mother, who'd returned with the party, studied her for a long moment. "Why are ye here? Yer husband, whether dead or alive, is gone."

It took every ounce of strength not to cry. Ava swallowed. "It was my fault that he was captured and hung."

Her uncle looked to them. "What was he accused of?"

"He killed guards, picked them off one by one. Some sort of vendetta," her mother answered, waving her hand as if it were nothing more than a nuisance. "I doubt it was him. It was probably one of our own guardsmen. They are not loyal. They should be hung, every one of them."

The guardsmen in the room looked to one another making Ava wonder why they'd remained to begin with. Her family mistreated everyone in their charge.

Atholl, who looked to be in his forties, with silver temples and a sharp jawline, narrowed his eyes. "Guardsmen should be treated well. After all, they are who protects the family and clan. I will speak to the men and ensure that if there is a conflict within them, it will be rectified straight away. There must be harmony within this clan if we are to stand a chance to survive."

If Atholl Mackenzie was as wise as he sounded, perhaps the clan was headed for the better.

Her mother straightened and placed a hand over her chest. "Of course. What I meant is that whoever is found guilty should hang…or be punished."

Her mother was flirting with the man. Ava coughed to hide her grimace. "Laird, may I ask if it is possible for me to remain here to live?"

"I would like to request the same," her mother interjected.

Her uncle considered them for a moment. "Lady Fraser, of course. This is yer home." His gaze scanned Ava's face. "I will send a scout to find out if yer husband lives. If he does, ye will return to Fraser Keep. If he is dead, then I will allow ye to remain here. I do require a wife."

Her eyes rounded and her mouth fell open. Had the man just insinuated he would marry her? Ava's throat dried up. Her mother's face turned bright red and she glared at Ava.

"Splendid idea," her uncle said. "Perhaps as laird, ye can remain alive, unlike the first two."

The men laughed and Ava wanted to throw a tankard at their heads.

"There is no need to send a scout." Ava stood and crossed her arms. "I will go find out myself. If my husband is dead, I will return, otherwise, I will remain." She had absolutely no desire to remain in the house with her family.

Her brother was dead, buried without more than a few words by the vicar. Most of their allies were gone and now they planned to marry her off again.

She stormed from the room. Behind her, she could hear her mother telling them how Ava had always been strong-willed and not very stable.

EARLY THE NEXT morning, Ava waited for the stable master to saddle her horse. "Do ye wish to take food for the beast, Miss Ava?" the man asked.

"Aye, thank ye." The trip would normally take a day, but

after her last trip, she wanted to be prepared. In a sack, she'd packed food, a separate set of clothes and a shawl. For protection, her short sword was strapped to her waist. Between her breasts, a dirk was hidden, and a second one was strapped to her right ankle. She'd taken plenty of coin from her brother's room. More than enough to survive for several years, if she was frugal.

Ava rode through the forest, stopping at the old woman's cottage. Quickly, she delivered a bundle that included food and some coins. She noticed wood had been chopped and placed under an overhang by her back door as she'd instructed.

Through the window, the woman spotted her and hurried outside. Her gray hair was askew as always. The cap she wore was unable to tame it. She gave Ava a toothy grin. "Ye always take such good care of me. I was hoping to see ye and thank ye for everything."

Ava made a mental note to find someone to bring the old woman supplies in the winter.

"Ye took care of me when I was a wee lass. Now it is my turn. I came to retrieve my items," Ava said, smiling.

She hurried behind the cottage and pulled a sack that was hidden under some broken pots. Upon returning to the door, Ava hugged the woman and mounted.

The trek to Fraser Keep would not take long. As a matter of fact, the dread of how she'd be received would probably make it seem short.

Ava pulled the hood of her cloak up and rode south.

BEHIND HER, THE sun fell below the horizon as she neared her destination. The closer Ava got to Fraser Keep, the harder her tears fell. It was almost impossible to see and hard to breathe as sobs racked her body. It wasn't herself she cried for, but the possibility that Keithen would not be there.

Guards at the gates exchanged perplexed looks when she approached and dismounted. Like most men, they were unsure what to do when a woman cried for no apparent reason. Someone hurried up and took her horse. On leaden feet, she trudged to the front door where Lady Fraser appeared. Esme stood next to her.

Keithen's mother took her arm and led her inside, while Esme hovered, seeming annoyed at her appearance. However, the woman must have taken pity on her, because she was silent.

"Where have ye been?" Lady Fraser asked. "Ye look a fright."

"I was abducted when riding back from Clan Ross. Then I managed to get away, went back to Mackenzie Keep, to see if Keithen…" She stopped speaking, unsure what to say.

"Ye stayed there then?" Esme's voice was hard.

"Aye, to nurse my brother until he died." She didn't meet the woman's stare, but noticed Esme look away. "I stayed with his body, pretending he was alive until family from the north arrived."

"Did ye even wonder about my brother?" Esme asked with a sneer.

Ava closed her eyes and swallowed. "Of course I did. No second passed that I did not wish to see him. Is he…?"

"He survived. Barely." Lady Fraser's words took a moment to sink in.

Her entire body went limp and she swayed.

"Come, sit down," Lady Fraser murmured, once again taking her arm. "Bring some mead," she ordered someone.

Moments later, a cup was pushed into her hand. Ava took a deep drink and placed it on the table. "I wish to see him."

The women exchanged looks but, finally, Lady Fraser nodded. "Of course. He is in yer chamber."

Hurrying up the steps, she only slowed upon reaching the door. Once there, she took a deep breath before entering.

The room was bright. Several lanterns were lit on multiple surfaces.

On the bed, her husband slept. Yellow and purple bruises covered most of his face and an angry red mark crossed his neck. She didn't know what other injuries there were since blankets were pulled up to his chest. Nearing the bed, she had to resist the urge to push a lock of hair away from his brow. Even battered, he was achingly handsome.

"Keithen." His name, just above a whisper, sounded strange on her lips.

His eyes fluttered and then opened. Upon seeing her, they widened. For a long moment, they looked into each other's eyes, not speaking. Finally, Ava reached for his shoulder and pressed her hand upon it.

"How are ye feeling?"

He gave a soft nod, then he let out a long breath. "Better now that I see ye. What happened?"

Unsure of how much to divulge in that moment, Ava skirted the question. "I was with my brother. He died."

"I cannot say I am sorry."

Everything was her fault. Keithen's injuries, Alastair's death and other things she wasn't prepared to think about.

"I know it was best for me not to come back. But I needed to know how ye fared."

Unsure she was strong enough to hear his recriminations, she continued without stopping. "Once I am sure ye are healing properly, I will leave." She lifted the blanket to find that his chest was bound tightly. *Broken ribs*.

His left leg was splinted from the knee down. A fracture that would undoubtedly leave him with a permanent limp. A cut on the right thigh had been stitched. Like his face, there were angry bruises all over.

Pulling up the blanket, she met his gaze. "Yer healer has done well."

"I have ye to thank for my life."

Ava shook her head. "How can ye say that? It was me that caused all of this to happen."

"Ye care for yer family and had to see about them."

"I have been so very foolish. Because of me, ye almost died."

His gaze lifted to her. "And because of ye, I live."

He paused for a moment. "Why did ye not return?"

The burden that she carried, the weight like that of a boulder upon her shoulders seemed to press down. "I was on my way back to Mackenzie Keep when I stopped to rest…"

Ava continued speaking, telling Keithen about her capture and then rescue by a woman named Hilda and the ultimate help by the man, Thomas. "I then went to the keep to find out what happened to ye and found that my brother was dying."

"Ye have been through a great deal." Keithen lifted a hand and she took it. "We will ensure that coin and what ye promised to the woman are sent," Keithen reassured her.

Ava nodded. "I owe her a great debt." She held her breath. "May I stay?"

CHAPTER NINETEEN

THANKFUL THAT NO one was in the room, Keithen slid from the bed and hobbled to the trunk at the foot of it. It took a bit of maneuvering, but he managed to pull out a tunic and then grabbed his tartan that hung on the door of the wardrobe and wrapped it around his waist. He pulled a corner up over his shoulders and belted it in place.

He waited a moment for the lightheadedness to go away and then hopped to the doorway. There was no time to remain in bed. If he was to recover faster, it was best to make himself move about and do more than remain in the bedchamber.

At the end of the corridor, he hesitated. The stairs would be hard to get down. One missed step and he would tumble.

"Do not move." Broden appeared at the bottom of the steps and held both hands up. He hurried up the stairs and helped Keithen down. It was slow progress, especially when his ribcage began aching, but they made it to the first floor.

There were a few people milling about the space. Two stood before his father, arguing, while another group waited to be heard.

Keithen allowed Broden to help him to the sideboard where he lowered to a chair. His father looked to him, acknowledged

Keithen with a nod and continued listening to the argument.

Once the situation between the men was resolved, the group who'd been waiting approached. They presented an idea for a multi-family farm that would share responsibilities of farming a parcel of land. They asked for land to farm and keep livestock on.

His father considered the request, conferring with two council members and, in the end, the land was granted to them.

Finally, Broden spoke. He reported on needs and requirements found while on patrol. The head archer, Ewan Ross, was next. He presented requests from the Ross guardsmen.

Keithen listened and gave input as needed.

Finally, a meal was served and as everyone ate, his father turned to him. "I am glad that ye are well enough to be here."

"Do we have many injuries from the attack on Mackenzie Keep?"

Broden spoke up. "Five men injured, no dead."

"One man injured, one dead," Ewan reported for the archers.

"Alastair Mackenzie is dead," Keithen told them, noting that everyone was surprised at the news. "Ava kept his death a secret until the Mackenzie from the north arrived. She said Atholl Mackenzie has been appointed as laird."

The council began discussing their thoughts on the new laird, while Keithen scanned the room for his wife.

"Father, may I speak to ye in private?"

With his father's help, they went to the study and closed the door. Keithen didn't sit. He needed to spend time upright.

"If this is about Ava, whether she will remain or not, I leave it up to ye to make that choice." His father paced. "She is yer wife and her ride to seek help is not only admirable, but it saved yer life. However, her recklessness is the reason for all of it. Ye almost dying. One archer dead."

"I am not sure what to do," Keithen admitted. "She is my wife and although her actions were wrong, I do understand why she did it."

His father shook his head. "She disobeyed ye."

Keithen considered his own rebellious actions and how hunting the men who'd hurt Catriona was why he was almost killed. How could he judge his own wife for something similar?

"I did hunt down those guards and kill them. Therefore, I am partly to blame for everything."

His father didn't seem surprised. "Ye disobeyed me then." It was not a question, but a statement and Keithen nodded.

"If Ava remains here, with me, will it be against yer wishes?"

His father frowned. "Ye made vows to the woman, which makes her a Fraser. I believe she should remain. If she is scorned by the clanspeople, it is because she brought it upon herself. It will be a long time, if ever, that they accept her as one of our own."

Needing time to think about what he'd say to Ava, Keithen went out the back door to where Ava had begun a small garden. The rain and chill in the air did not seem to affect the herbs that grew tall now.

Ava was hunched over the patch, putting down wood shavings around the plants. Sensing his approach, she looked up and then jumped to her feet. "Ye are up. I am not sure ye should be about."

"I am fine."

Rubbing her hands on the apron she wore, his wife looked around. "Ye should sit."

"I would rather stand. It feels oddly good to do so."

"Ye have been avoiding me the last two days. We should talk," Keithen started. "There is much to discuss."

Ava nodded. "Other than admitting my blame for everything, what else do we have to speak about?" She looked everywhere but at him. "I must accept my fate of not being liked. Other than that, I suppose ye wish to speak of where I will sleep from now on."

"Where have ye been sleeping?"

She motioned up to a window. "Catriona has been kind enough to share her room with me. I have a cot in there."

"Ye will return to our bedchamber," Keithen said. "Ye are my wife, Ava. Nothing changes that."

When her shoulders rounded, and with a look of defeat, Keithen knew she carried a heavy burden. "Ava, there is nothing we can do to change the past. We must move forward."

Ava swallowed but didn't respond.

"Ye didn't answer my question before about what happened after ye fell behind. Why did Gallant return here?"

"I prefer not to speak of it." Ava rounded him and raced into the house.

LAST MEAL WAS subdued. Esme, Ruari and their guards had left earlier that day. There were guards seated at the tables since villagers and farmers who'd come to speak to his father had hurried home when storm clouds converged.

Beside him, Ava was quiet, but ate everything he'd placed on her plate.

"I am happy that ye join us for last meal," his mother said, smiling in his direction. "Ye must accept help getting back upstairs."

Keithen nodded. "I will."

Several guards began having a loud discussion followed by laughter. His father called out for them to share what they spoke of. One was voted spokesman and he neared the high board.

"Laird, there was an occurrence while we rode back from the southern borders of the land," he recounted. "We stopped for Finn to relieve himself. Ye see, a wee beast appeared out of nowhere, a rabbit perhaps. It scampered into the woods. Whatever the beastie did, it must have been terrible because Finn ran out screaming, his trews half-down." The man began laughing so hard, he could barely recount the rest of the story. Apparently, the small creature had scared Finn so badly, the man had tripped over his own clothing and then crawled to his horse.

Everyone joined in the laughter, much to poor Finn's expense. But the man took it with good nature and, after a while, he began telling his version.

Keithen noticed that although Ava listened, she didn't laugh. His mother wiped tears of mirth from the corners of her eyes and even Catriona chuckled softly.

"Over time, things like this will be what the people remember. Ye will have to be patient."

Ava turned to him and nodded, but there were doubts in her eyes.

At the end of the meal, she helped him maneuver the steps, which he hopped up. By the time they'd managed the last couple, both were out of breath.

Keithen had to take shallow breaths to keep from hurting, but it did not deter him from knowing he'd go back down the following day.

Once inside the bedchamber, Ava helped him remove the tartan, but he chose to keep the tunic on. Lifting his arms was not worth the pain in his opinion.

After undressing, she went to the bed wearing only her shift. Immediately, Keithen wished he didn't have the confines of a leg brace and aching ribs. His member hardened and he blew out a breath. This wasn't the time.

"I will help ye lie down. After, some whisky will help with the pain and allow ye to sleep more comfortably."

Her hands around him as she guided him to the bed was the last thing Keithen needed. He blew out a breath after managing to sit on the bed and swinging his legs sideways.

The tunic shifted upward, exposing him from the waist down. His staff jutted up like a tree, hard and proud.

Ava looked to him, her face turning a bright shade of pink. "Do ye wish to sit or lay flat?"

"Sit," he replied and purposefully made it hard for her to help slide him upward. Her face next to him as she pulled him up from under his arms was the closest they'd been in a long while.

"Ava," Keithen whispered.

She turned, and he took her mouth.

At first, she was reluctant and then slowly relaxed and wrapped her arms around his neck, kissing him back. It felt like all was right with the world in those moments as they savored each other as, finally, their tongues intermingled.

Ava was careful, lowering only enough to lay beside him, never allowing the kiss to break. She laid precariously on her side on the edge of the bed, but with his arm around her keeping her in place, she would not fall.

"I am so sorry," she whispered against his lips and Keithen took her mouth again, not wishing to hear regrets. He needed her close, to feel himself come to life with want was a reminder that he'd survived. Although he'd never feared death, what happened to him had been a stark slap of reality he had not been prepared for.

His thoughts lifted and disappeared when Ava's hand wrapped around his hardness. She stroked him from sack to tip, until he fought to breathe evenly.

"Mmmmm." Keithen pushed his head back against the pillows, doing his best not to breathe too deeply. Ava pressed her lips against his jaw and then trailed her tongue down the side of his neck, all the while maintaining a steady stroking rhythm, her hand sliding up and down his hard cock.

"Awww," Keithen moaned and covered her hand with his to guide her to move faster as his climax neared.

His release was strong and so hard the entire room went dark. He let out short hard breaths attempting to regain control.

Ava kissed him and slipped from the bed. "I will get yer whisky."

Too languid to try to move, he kept his eyes closed, opening them only when a glass was pressed to his lips and the woodsy scent tickled his nose.

"Ye should sleep well now," Ava said with a soft smile and pressed a kiss to his lips.

He drank the liquid, and immediately its effects lulled him into slumber. "Lay with me."

It was moments later that the bed dipped as she slipped into the bed, ensuring to keep distance between them.

TWICE, HIS WIFE had evaded telling him what happened to her. He had suspicions, especially when he tried to touch her in bed, and she would not allow more than kissing. Ava was hiding something and he needed to know what it was.

It was early one afternoon when his mother joined him in the courtyard. He stood away from where the guards and his father practiced at swordplay.

"I wish they would not be so violent," his mother said with a shudder. "I came to find ye. The healer said yer stitches can be removed. Why did ye not remain for him to do so?"

"Ava can do it later," Keithen replied. "I had to be at a council meeting."

"How is she?" his mother asked. "She has not joined Catriona and me in the sitting room."

Keithen shrugged. "I feel she is still uncomfortable after all that has happened."

"Poor lass. Especially after her harrowing experience at the hands of ruffians."

His chest constricted. "What do ye speak of?"

"Did she not tell ye?" When he shook his head, his mother continued. "Upon arriving, she was in a horrible state, crying and very upset. Esme asked where she'd been, and Ava admitted to being at Mackenzie Keep after escaping being abducted." His mother sighed. "I cannot imagine what she's been through. Although I must agree in part with Esme. This was all of her own doing."

He already knew that part. What he didn't know was what else she was hiding. He touched his mother's shoulder. "I must go inside."

"I will help ye." His mother tried to help him but, in the end, two guards hurried over and helped him to the great room.

"Mother, will ye find Ava and tell her to come speak to me in

Father's study?" Lady Fraser nodded and went up the steps, her gaze moving back to him one last time before she disappeared.

He managed his way alone to his father's empty study and moments later, Ava entered.

"Yer mother says to remove yer stitches." She neared. "I can do it in our bedchamber later, after last meal."

"That will be fine," he replied. "We must talk."

Her nod was hesitant. "Very well."

"Ava, tell me what happed when ye were abducted? Mother told me ye admitted to it happening."

For a moment, he thought she was going to faint. All blood left her face, she paled, and her right hand lifted and lowered without reason. Ava's eyelids fluttered and closed for a moment, but she quickly recovered and turned away.

"There is nothing to tell. I escaped and found my way back."

Keithen wanted to shake her. Instead, he closed the distance between them and lifted her face. "Tell me the truth. Every detail. I need to hear it."

"What does it matter?" Ava snapped and took a step back. "I wish to forget about it."

"Something happened."

Despite the silence that followed, Keithen refused to relent. Whatever had happened, his wife would tell him. They were not going to leave the room until she did.

Seeming to sense he would not yield, Ava sat down and slumped forward onto the table, her face in her hands.

"After riding to Ross Keep all night, on the way to Mackenzie Keep, I could no longer keep up. Exhausted, I found what I thought was a safe place to sleep for a couple of hours."

Her voice was hollow as she continued. "I had fallen asleep. It was still dark when I heard Gallant making noise. They tried to take him, but yer horse is not exactly docile. Then one of them saw me. They stopped struggling with Gallant and came to me instead." She lifted her face and stared forward with an unfocused expression.

"I fought, but the two men overpowered me easily. One groped me, tore open my top. The other reached between my legs. But in the end, they did not do more than that. They had decided to sell me." Her eyes flickered to him. "They did not rape me, I was bleeding."

She took a long breath and Keithen remained silent, not wishing to stop her.

"For days, I was in a cramped wooden crate, gagged and tied. Relieved myself, bled and threw up. I must have looked and smelled horrible, because they decided to abandon the crate, with me in it, on the docks." She squeezed her eyes shut. "An old woman found me, took me to a man, who then I paid to bring me back."

The chair creaked when she stood and walked to the hearth. Visibly shaking, Ava held her hands out to the fire. "My captors were obviously inept to not have thought to search me for coin."

Taking everything in, Keithen sensed she was still withholding something. "I am grateful ye were not hurt worse. I do not blame ye for what happened, Ava."

She stood very still and let out a long breath. As much as he wanted to go to her, Keithen felt it had to be her decision. "I do not wish to be forgiven or accepted. I do not expect to be treated kindly. I do not deserve it."

"Why do ye feel so strongly about it?"

"Ye came close to death. It was my fault that ye were hung and continue to suffer. It is my fault my brother is dead." Ava's voice trembled as she spoke, her shoulders shaking. "I killed our child."

Her knees seemed to buckle, and she crumbled to the floor. Keithen remained standing as, with his injuries, he could not lower.

Instead, he moved closer and stood next to her. "Ye lost a bairn?"

"Because I had to go. Because I went to see if my mother and brother were injured. They would have never done the same for me. They were not appreciative and acted as if I was there to spy for yer father." She wasn't crying. It was more as if she'd given up. "I was not going to return. However, I realize that I deserve every mistreatment from Clan Fraser. I deserve the worst."

"Ye are not going to be mistreated, Ava." Keithen had yet to absorb the reality of what she'd disclosed. He was going to be a father. If she'd not gone to her family, then he would not have been captured, and she'd not have gone through the abduction.

"Laird Mackenzie was intent on blaming the death of those guards on a Fraser. They would have captured me or another Fraser eventually. Catriona's attack…" he began.

"Ye and she should have been who married. If only my father had not intervened," she interrupted.

"Ava…"

"No." Ava jumped to her feet and ran from the room.

"WHAT HAPPENED?" HIS father entered the room.

Keithen told him everything. Mostly because repeating it helped him understand it himself. "I am not sure how I feel in this moment."

Laird Fraser poured two glasses of whisky and handed him one. "The only thing ye can do is allow time to pass. Ye need to heal and yer wife does as well."

"She blames herself for everything, and although it is partially true, I am to blame as well for my continued quest of revenge."

"Rebelliousness is not without consequences," his father said, and Keithen realized the deep truth. He'd rebelled against his father and sought to get revenge and now his own child had paid the price.

His father placed a hand on Keithen's shoulder. "Learn this, my son. There is a time and a place for everything. The first reaction is not always the right one."

Keithen nodded. He slogged out of the room and, upon noting the long corridor in front, he motioned a servant over. "Help me get to Miss Catriona's room."

"KEITHEN," CATRIONA HURRIED to help him into the room. The door remained open as she helped him to sit and then brought a stool to rest his leg on. She studied him. "Ye look unwell."

"Bring some mead and ask Eileen to make some meat broth." When the servant hurried away, she turned back to him. "Ye should not be about so much."

He studied his friend and, as always, his heart broke at considering what she'd endured at the hands of the Mackenzie's guardsmen. Months later, scars on her neck remained. Since her return, she wore a high collar on her gowns, which made him aware there had to be many others hidden.

"Why are ye here?" Catriona asked. "Do ye need to talk?"

He nodded. "I need to ask ye some things."

"Very well." Catriona lowered to a second chair. "What is it?"

"Years ago, Esme told me ye were in love with me. Because I knew I was destined to marry someone my father chose, I made every effort to not give ye hope."

Catriona's expression barely changed. She waited for him to continue.

"I wish that I could say I felt the same way. I have always loved ye dearly, but only as a sister," Keithen continued. "And now I question it. Mainly because I brought so much pain and disaster to our door because I was driven mad with the need to avenge what happened to ye. I have been killing every man that touched ye."

This time, Catriona reacted, her eyes widening. She knew this but was still surprised by his admission. "Oh…" she hesitated and swallowed. "Oh, Keithen." Her eyes filled with sadness.

"I went against my father's orders and now I learn Ava lost our child because she rode so far to try to save my life." He hung his head, defeated. "I am not sure what to do or how to feel. What should I feel?" He fought to keep tears from spilling.

Catriona met his gaze. "Angry, hurt and betrayed. Ye acted out of love. Ye would have done the same if it were Esme who was mistreated."

He acknowledged it was true. For Esme, he would have killed them all.

She hesitated and took his hand. "Darling, what Esme said was true. Ye have always been the man I loved. Ye are the bravest man I have ever known."

Footsteps sounded, probably the servant, but no one entered.

Catriona continued. "Despite how I felt about ye, now when I see ye and Ava together, I understand the true meaning of fate."

"Why would fate bring us together? To what end?" Keithen asked, too angry to keep his voice down.

"Because there is no ye without her in yer life now. Admit it."

AVA WALKED DOWN the corridor holding two glasses of mead. She'd intercepted a servant heading for Catriona's room and taken the drinks as an excuse to speak to her. Upon reaching the doorway, she'd stopped at hearing Catriona's voice. She'd been professing her love to Keithen.

What she'd said was not meant for anyone other than Keithen's ears.

"Take these to Miss Catriona," she told the confused servant she'd taken the glasses from just moments ago.

CHAPTER TWENTY

AVA'S CHEST EXPANDED almost to a painful point with each breath. Her child was gone. For days, she'd kept the thought at bay, blocking out what had occurred, the true reason for all the blood. But now that she'd spoken the words, it was as if a knife had been thrust into her chest and sliced it open.

Life had always been cruel to her and she'd accepted it. However, for things to go so far, losing a child was more than she could bear.

"Ava." Lady Fraser walked out and upon seeing her crying neared. "Did Keithen do something?"

Ava shook her head. "I admitted everything to him." Exhausted, she leaned on the short wall that surrounded the area. "Have ye ever felt as if ye cannot possibly go on?"

"I think everyone does at some point. There are so many things that can happen. But ye know, it is best at times not to think on it too much."

As much as Ava liked the woman, Lady Fraser seemed to never dwell on things. The lady expertly avoided situations that she considered "not a woman's concern".

"I think what we need is a distraction. Now that Keithen is better, we will go visit the Frasers across the river. Spend a few weeks there before it becomes too cold to travel."

"Visit?" Ava was shocked. "Ye are going away?"

"We are. Ye and I will go. Perhaps Catriona as well. I hope ye will help me convince her." Lady Fraser looked up at the cloudy sky. "Once winter arrives, we will be stuck indoors for days on end."

"I do not believe they will wish to have me visit." Ava had to admit the woman had managed to distract her from self-pity.

Lady Fraser gave a halfhearted wave. "The invitation was addressed to us both."

For a moment, Ava was stunned. The Frasers acted as if she was, indeed, one of them. As much as she wanted to turn down the invitation, her curiosity was piqued. "I will have to speak to Keithen. Although at the moment, he is probably too angry with me to hear what I have to say."

"Keithen is very patient."

"I lost our bairn. When I was taken."

"Oh, dear." Lady Fraser came to her and hugged her. "I am so truly sorry."

The woman's lack of judgment and the fact she actually hugged her was foreign to Ava. The feeling was like being surrounded by sunshine.

"Now," Lady Fraser said moving away. "Wipe yer tears and see about asking yer husband. I am sure Keithen will agree that ye need a distraction."

"I need a few moments to compose myself. I will consider yer invitation. Thank ye."

When she was finally alone, Ava considered everything that had happened. She doubted that Keithen would forgive her for what happened. Winter was approaching and like Lady Fraser had said, they would be forced to spend many days indoors. She wondered what she should do. On one hand, to leave would be a good distraction, but Keithen was still recovering and needed help to complete tasks.

She opened a gate and went through it carrying a bucket. It

hadn't rained in several days, so she decided to water her herb garden. At the well, several women were gathered and, for a moment, Ava hesitated.

As the laird's son's wife, they would not openly do or say anything, but that would not stop them from glaring. Ava took a breath and walked to the well.

"Lady Ava," one woman said as she approached and lowered her head in a slight bow in greeting. "How fares yer husband from the injuries caused by yer family?"

"He is recovering well," Ava answered, looking to the other women. "Thank ye for yer concern."

An older woman met her gaze. "Yer clan has been to blame for many a death. We wish to ensure that we don't lose our laird's son as well."

It would have been better if they had remained silent as there were heavy implications in every word.

"I, too, do not wish to lose my husband and am doing everything I possibly can to ensure he recovers." Ava turned the crank bringing up water and then reached for the bucket to pour into hers.

A woman about her age pretended to stumble and kicked it out of the way just as she poured water into it.

"I do apologize," she said in a flat voice and, along with the other women, she walked away murmuring not so softly.

"Why did she bother to return?"

"Hopefully, she will leave again and not return," said another.

Flora hurried over. "That group is nothing but a bunch of gossips. Do not pay them any heed."

Ava straightened her bucket and then drew more water from the well. "I do not plan to leave. I will remain and care for Keithen and fulfill all my duties."

"Lady Fraser said she invited ye to go with her to visit the other Frasers," Flora said. "Will ye not go then?"

As they walked back to her herb garden, Flora explained that Catriona was not going. "She does not feel up to traveling yet.

Although she has made good progress, she cannot fathom traveling as yet."

Upon seeing that she carried a bucket, a young guard hurried over and took it from her. "Miss Ava, ye can ask for our help for things like this." He whistled while carrying the bucket and then placed it on the ground next to her garden patch.

The guard left to continue whatever tasks he had to do, and Ava wondered if it was only the women that did not want her there.

"Flora, do ye think the men are more forgiving of me?"

"I think the women are angrier that ye married Keithen and use yer family as a good excuse to express their disappointment."

There were so many questions Ava wanted to ask, but she was not sure Flora would tell her. As she had no one else to ask, she decided it was best to take a chance.

"I must ask, were there plans for Keithen to marry someone else before his father and mine interceded?"

Flora shrugged. "It was common knowledge his marriage would be an arranged one. However, like most men, he did have a few entanglements here and there."

"With the woman who kicked my bucket?"

"Gracious, that would explain her ire." Flora giggled. "I am not sure. I doubt it."

Ava took a breath. "What about Catriona?"

At the question, Flora's eyes widened. She looked to the doorway as if she expected to be overheard. "Why would ye ask that?"

"Because I know she has deep feelings for him."

Flora frowned. "He and Catriona have been very close since they were children. It was rare to see one without the other. When they became older, Catriona then became closer with Esme. She and Keithen, however, have always been confidantes."

Flora hesitated. "Up until she was captured. It took a while before he could go near her."

"Were they ever more than friends?" Ava pushed, hoping

Flora could somehow clarify what she'd heard earlier.

"I do not know. It may be best that ye ask her directly. As his wife, ye have a right to."

Ava considered it. "I do not wish to cause her any undue anxiousness. It is just that I wish to know because of things I have heard."

Thankfully, Flora didn't ask what she'd heard or where. The woman was not only kind, but wise. "I understand," she said.

"I must find Lady Fraser and tell her I will not be traveling with her. Do ye think she will be cross?"

Flora shook her head. "I am sure she will find someone else to travel with her. The laird's brother's wife likes to go with her."

When Flora turned to the bucket, Ava stopped her with a hand to her upper arm. "Thank ye for being so kind to me. If anyone has reason not to care for me, it is ye. I can only hope to be able to repay ye."

"What happened is not yer fault. Although I understand the bitterness of people who've lost loved ones through battles between our clans, I do not agree with blaming ye. Yer father's decisions were not yers."

Ava nodded. "Ye, Catriona and Lady Fraser have made my living here bearable. I hate that she is leaving because I am not sure the staff will obey me when I oversee her tasks. It will definitely be a task just to get them to do as they are told."

"Ye should talk to Lady Fraser and ensure she speaks to them before leaving," Flora said and took her hand. "Come, let us go find her now. I wager she is with Catriona."

Ava was glad that Keithen was not in Catriona's bedchamber when they arrived.

Lady Fraser turned to them as they walked in. "I am sure we can convince Flora to come and then ye will have company. The ride across the river is delightful."

It felt strange to be in Catriona's bedchamber after having heard her profess her love to her husband. Ava hovered near the doorway. "I have decided not to go," she blurted.

"By the middle of winter, ye will wish to have had a distraction," Lady Fraser said, sounding annoyed. "Very well. Ye all can stay here. I am going."

"I must speak to ye about taking over yer duties," Ava said, noting that Lady Fraser's eyebrows shot up.

"Of course. I hadn't considered that ye would need tutelage." Lady Fraser clasped her hands in front of her chest with a gleeful expression. "We shall walk through the keep and I will tell ye everything."

Before Ava could say anything else, Lady Fraser took her arm. "Come along, this will take all day. First, we will go to the kitchen."

Ava was sure that because Lady Fraser accompanied her, the head cook, Eileen, was cordial. Along with the four cooks, the woman stood around the preparation table to listen.

"I am traveling for an extended time, a fortnight. Lady Ava will be taking my place and will give ye instructions to what will be served. Ensure that ye obey her instructions or I will be very cross with ye."

Every head turned to Ava and she was relieved to see no animosity. "I am sure ye will require little guidance as Lady Fraser assures me of yer competence."

When everyone returned their attention to Lady Fraser, her expression softened. "The guardsmen will be eating inside from now on as the weather turns colder. Send someone to the village to alert the baker to bring extra bread as with all the cooking, ye will not have time to bake for first and last meal."

Ava listened to every word that was exchanged. Although she'd helped her mother with running of the keep, the requirements at Fraser Keep were much more complicated. Not only because they fed more people, but also two separate meals were to be served. The guardsmen were to be divided into two separate groups, so that everyone would fit in the great room.

"What will ye be serving?" Ava asked the cook.

"Today, we are making mutton and leek stew, which can be

stretched far to ensure everyone eats enough to be full. There will be bread, cheese and figs as well."

"It smells delicious," Ava said.

Eileen preened. "It does, indeed, and it tastes very good."

They made their way to adjoining rooms that opened to the outdoors. There, a team of maids washed soiled clothing and linens while others mended. One young maid stirred a pot over an open fire, her brow scrunched in concentration.

Lady Fraser held her hands up to get their attention and again informed the group of her upcoming travels. Ava stood by, curious to see what their reactions would be to Lady Fraser leaving her in charge. The maids seemed more interested in finding out where their mistress was traveling than in Ava's taking over the responsibilities.

It seemed Lady Fraser had a good rapport with the servants. They were genuinely curious about where she would travel, what her destination looked like and another host of things. It took considerably longer to get away from the laundresses than the cooks.

Ava was pleasantly surprised when they went out to the corrals where Lady Fraser spoke to an older man who was in charge of a pen of goats and two cows. Apparently, he was very protective of the animals, not allowing them to be considered for eating. His animals were purely used for their milk.

In the pen with the cows was a doe, who looked quite at home amidst the others. Ava wondered if the old man's poor eyesight made him think it was a goat.

"Why is there a deer in the pen?" she whispered to Lady Fraser.

The old man obviously had keen ears. "That is Esme's pet doe, Dot."

"We tried to release her," Lady Fraser explained. "But she kept returning, so now she remains here. The animal seems content enough."

As they made their way to find the servants who cleaned the

keep, Ava noticed that there were not as many people in the courtyard as usual.

"Esme will never forgive me, nor will she accept me as part of this clan." Ava's throat constricted. "I understand, of course, however, I hope that one day she will."

Lips curving into a soft smile, Lady Fraser slid a look to her. "Esme is very headstrong. Much too adventurous for a woman. In that, ye remind me of her. I believe, in time, ye will become friends."

She seriously doubted that Keithen's sister and she would be friends, however, she hoped to be on better terms with her, eventually.

"That reminds me," Lady Fraser said. "I wish for ye to look after Catriona's well-being. Flora is wonderful and Catriona's mother visits often, but some nights she has horrible nightmares and the day after barely eats. I cannot imagine what the poor lass went through." Lady Fraser shuddered.

"Do not worry. I will ensure to spend time with her every day."

"In the sitting room. She must leave her room and not remain in her own room the entire time."

Ava decided it was the perfect opportunity to bring up what she'd overheard. "All of ye hold Catriona in high regard. It would seem to me, a marriage between her and Keithen would have been something that would have pleased ye."

Lady Fraser chuckled. "I'd not thought of it. Of course, the poor girl pined for Keithen since she was very young. Our son has always known he will marry based on becoming laird one day, so he never gave her hope."

"I find that sad. I am sure Catriona must have been heartbroken when we married."

Lady Fraser studied her for a moment. "I do not remember her being particularly sad. Esme would know better. Everyone was in a bit of a shock that he was to marry a Mackenzie."

"Of course," Ava acknowledged, a familiar pang in the pit of her stomach. "I was the last person ye would wish for yer son."

With a soft chuckle, Lady Fraser patted her arm. "I would not go that far. I do find ye and my son to be quite compatible, if not too much alike. Both of ye have a rebellious nature, which brings trouble."

When the group of cleaning servants were assembled, Lady Fraser spent several minutes asking about their families and inquiring if one of them, who was not present, had given birth yet. She turned to Ava. "We must ensure to send a basket with food and a blanket I embroidered for the wee one."

Ava was astonished at how much Lady Fraser not only took care of on a daily basis, but the fact she knew each member of the staff so well. Once she had a free moment, she vowed to sit down and write notes so to remember what had transpired.

Once again, Lady Fraser spoke to the staff about her upcoming travel and answered some of the same questions that the others had asked. She promised to bring regards to relatives, which delighted several.

By the time they sat in the sitting room and drank hot cider, Ava was overwhelmed. "I must admit to being impressed by ye. The staff respects and cares for ye."

Lady Fraser nodded. "It is an interdependence, Ava. We depend on the servants for our well-being. Everything from eating to our clothing and horses. In turn, they depend on us to have a purpose and a means to support their families."

The staff at Mackenzie Keep was kept to a minimum. Although she knew the names of the cook and her chambermaid, her mother had insisted that they keep them at arm's length. Servants were dismissed constantly for the most minimal of infractions. Some days, they had only one or two to do a myriad of tasks.

"When do ye leave?" Ava asked, not sure she was prepared for the huge undertaking.

"Three days hence," Lady Fraser replied, placing her cup down. "Tomorrow, I will begin packing and send a message to

Matilde," she said, referring to her husband's brother's wife. "I will make sure she has begun to pack as well."

LAST MEAL WAS crowded, but everything went according to plan. Ava studied how the meal was served to each person and once they finished, bowls were quickly taken away so they would not linger. Those that attended second meal had more time to linger, but they did not stay very long. Only those who slept inside the keep and a few visitors remained.

Keithen sat next to her. He'd been in deep conversation with the laird and a council member for most of the meal. Because Lady Fraser kept a constant commentary, pointing out items she considered important to be brought up to the staff, Ava could not hear what Keithen and the laird spoke about.

When Ava yawned, Keithen turned to her. "Ye should go to bed. I will join ye after a while."

She had much to speak to him about, but it would have to wait as he showed no intention of going upstairs at the moment.

Instead of going directly to bed, Ava moved to sit next to Lady Fraser.

"Let us join Catriona," Lady Fraser insisted. "She is not yet fully comfortable being in the great room."

They went to the small table and sat down. Catriona gave them a relieved smile. "I was about to leave. I am trying to remain, but it is difficult." She looked over her shoulder. "With the guardsmen inside now, it's..." She didn't have to finish.

Ava noted the woman had barely touched her food but refrained from saying anything about it.

"Have ye reconsidered coming with me?" Lady Fraser asked. "I do believe it will be helpful to ye and to Ava as well."

"What do ye mean?" Catriona asked.

Ava did her best not to gawk at the woman. Was Lady Fraser about to disclose her insecurities when it came to Catriona and Keithen?

"Just that it will give Ava the opportunity to be Lady of the

Keep and Keithen to act as laird."

"My responsibilities are minimal. I do not plan to intervene in anything," Catriona assured them. "I would not be averse to remaining in my bedchamber the entire time ye are gone."

Relieved, Ava let out a breath. "I would actually prefer if ye remain. If I have any questions, I will come to ye."

Obviously relieved, Catriona nodded. "It is doubtful that I can be of much assistance. My duties are minimal. However, I will help where I can."

There had never been anything but kindness toward her from Catriona. Ava wondered how it was possible for the woman not to hate her. From what she'd heard, she'd loved Keithen for years.

It could be that she and Keithen were both in love and had accepted that he had to be married. Her mind reeled at the thought that they had been, and continued to be, lovers. Ava gasped and the other women turned to her.

"What is wrong?" Lady Fraser asked.

"I think some sort of insect crawled over my arm." Ava shook her arm dramatically and wiped her hand down it. "It was probably just my imagination."

"They are coming indoors with the weather turning so cold outside," Catriona explained. "I do not care for it myself."

Surprisingly, Keithen came to bed just a few moments after Ava. He was quiet as he undressed and washed his face in the basin. "Mother is leaving for a long visit to my uncle's. She told me ye plan to take over her duties."

"Do ye approve?" Ava studied him closely, attempting to read his expression. If she was going to succeed in running the household, she would need his support.

He nodded. "Aye, of course. But ye must be prepared for some resistance. Stay firm."

"Please do not intervene on my behalf. I will have to do this myself."

"Come to me if ye need me."

Keithen tipped her chin up so she could meet his gaze. "Do ye want to talk about the bairn?"

Instantly, her eyes welled and her chest constricted. All the things she'd kept in check threatened to break through, and Ava wasn't sure she could control the myriad of emotions.

She shook her head. "I cannot."

"Ye must at some point," Keithen urged. "We both should."

After pulling her against his chest, he stroked her hair. "I never considered bairns. I suppose most men think of having a son. But for some reason, it had not occurred to me."

"Children are gifts from God. I feel as if I rejected it by my actions." The dam broke and, unable to keep from it, Ava wailed. She cried, mourning the loss of her child as a consequence of her actions. She grieved for her father, her brother and for the loss of a family she never quite had.

Through it all, Keithen held her and brought a cloth so that she could blow her nose and wipe away the tears. Finally, exhausted, Ava slumped forward.

In a strange way, she felt cleansed, free.

"Ye are an exceptional woman. Do not ever allow yerself to think otherwise," Keithen told her, his arms coming around her like a warm breeze.

"Yer words and body soothe me."

She looked up at him, loving the man so much her entire being ached. "I am hopeful we will have several children. And yet, I prefer it to happen after I'm accepted by the clan. It would be horrible for our children to be mistreated in any way."

"There is time. I do not doubt ye will win the people over."

Despite everything that had occurred, hope filled her heart.

JUST TWO DAYS after Lady Fraser left, Ava was ready to give up. "I instructed ye to sweep up the rushes so they can be replaced.

Why has that not been accomplished?" Ava pinned a pair of maids with her best annoyed look.

With a pinched expression, one of them shrugged. "Ye never told us to sweep them, Mistress. Ye just said lay out new rushes."

"It goes without saying the old ones should be gathered up and thrown out prior to new ones being spread."

"We do as we're told," the second one piped up.

Then both maids scurried away before she could say another word. Ava turned to study the great room. It was a horrible mess. New rushes thrown over old ones, the tables had yet to be cleaned and, to top it off, Laird Fraser was holding a council meeting as cook's maids attempted to carry trays without tripping on the mounds of rushes.

Keithen, who sat next to his father, looked over to her. Concern was evident in his expression, but as she'd asked him not to intervene, he didn't.

She stomped after the maids and caught them giggling in the corridor, just outside the kitchen.

"Come with me. Now." She gritted the words out, glad to see their wide-eyed expressions.

Both of them followed her to a small alcove. "Each of ye, get a broom." They did as they were told.

Ava pointed toward the great room. "If I must show ye how to sweep in front of the laird, I will do it." She grabbed a broom and stalked forward.

The maids looked to each other as if trying to decide what to do, but then hurried in front of her as she did not hesitate.

Once in the great room, Ava held the broom in both hands and swept sideways. "This is how ye sweep," she said loudly. "Make piles, which ye will then put in buckets and carry out to lay onto the garden."

She met each maid's glare. "I will watch ye to ensure ye know how to sweep. If ye do not, then we can see about replacing ye."

"Ye cannot," one replied. "My family has worked for the laird for generations."

"A generation can be skipped," Ava replied.

The maids began sweeping while Ava stood by.

She looked over to Keithen and the corners of his lips twitched. Ava pressed her lips together to keep from smiling.

CHAPTER TWENTY-ONE

KEITHEN MISSED BEING outdoors and riding his horse. Although it had been three weeks since his return from capture, he was still having a hard time maneuvering. It was most cumbersome to have a broken leg. Thankfully, he was mobile, albeit with help most times.

Upon seeing him standing outside the corral, Gallant neared and nudged his shoulder, expecting a treat. Keithen pulled a sweet turnip from his pocket, gave it to his steed and watched the animal eat.

"Ye will not be able to ride for a long while yet," Ewan told him as the archer approached.

Keithen nodded. "I do not like not doing my duties. There is always much to be done before winter sets in."

"My men have been given new tasks." Ewan looked over his shoulder. "There are rumblings that the new Laird Mackenzie is as bad as the last when it comes to ambition and seeking power over smaller clans."

"Aye, I have heard," Keithen replied. "It must be in their blood, the lust for overtaking and destruction."

Just then, Broden and his team rode through the gates. One of the guardsmen was slumped over, being held up by another man.

Keithen and Ewan hurried closer.

"What happened?" Keithen asked as the injured man was lowered from the horse.

Broden turned to another man. "Fetch the healer. Hurry!" He then looked to Keithen. "Someone shot at us. We were lucky to have an archer with us, who shot back at the trees so we could escape. I can only assume he was a Mackenzie since we were close to their lands when it happened."

"That makes little sense. Why would they provoke us?" Keithen shook his. "Perhaps someone is angry about the laird's death and blames us for it."

"There is no way to know," Broden said and hurried to where the injured man was taken.

Annoyed at the injury, Keithen remained in the courtyard. Whoever had attacked the patrol could have been hunting for him. After all, he usually went with that group. Perhaps the Mackenzies were not aware of his broken leg and assumed he was back to his regular duties.

From the doorway, his father motioned for him to come inside. Keithen knew they'd be discussing the same thing he'd been thinking.

They would never be friends with the Mackenzie, but perhaps it was time for them to meet and find out exactly where they stood.

"We will send a messenger to the new laird," Laird Fraser said. "We'll ask for a meeting before winter sets in."

"I wish to go," Keithen said. "I should be there."

His father shook his head. "And remind them that because of yer rescue the last laird was killed? It makes little sense."

Keithen clamped down his teeth to keep from cursing.

"We should bring a show of force to this meeting, which I believe should be held where the lands meet," a councilman stated.

Broden blew out a breath. "I wonder how large the Mackenzie's army is now. He lost many men when his allies broke away."

"How does Keithen and Ava's marriage affect our relationship with them?" Ewan asked.

Laird Fraser considered the question for a long moment. "I am not sure, as they tried to hang my son and accused him of killing the laird and guardsmen."

KEITHEN'S LEG ACHED, but it wasn't as bad as he'd expected. He'd managed to get his father to agree to him riding with the guardsmen that would accompany the laird to meet with the new Mackenzie. The only thing was that Keithen was to remain in the back with the archers.

Next to him, Ewan sat straight as the two lairds, flanked by two guards each, rode to meet in the center of an open area.

Behind the lairds, their armies lined up in rows, every man looking across the field to the other side. Every one of them measuring and counting.

From what Keithen could see, the Mackenzie must have brought every man he could gather. There were about two hundred, but it was evident some of them were not warriors. It was easy to tell by the way they had a hard time keeping their horses still.

Keithen huffed under his breath knowing the Fraser army was three hundred and it didn't count the men they'd left behind to guard the keep.

He hated not being at his father's side the way it should be. The first-born son was always at his father's side during times like this. Instead, Broden and his uncle flanked the laird.

Laird Mackenzie was slender. By his dark hair, he looked much younger than Keithen's father. He rode a black horse and wore the Mackenzie tartan, which was pulled over his shoulder and pinned in place by the Mackenzie Clan crest, if Keithen had to guess.

The conversation continued for longer than anyone expected.

"Seems the Mackenzie is not pleased," Ewan said, craning his neck. "By the way he's gesturing, he is not satisfied with the direction of the conversation."

"I agree," Keithen said and studied the men in the Mackenzie front lines to ensure none made any sudden moves. It seemed everyone thought the same, because the guardsmen in front of him seemed to all lean forward just enough that it was noticeable.

Ewan turned to him. "I do not think he is stupid enough to start anything. It is obvious we are a much stronger force."

Finally, the lairds turned away from each other. Each army parted, allowing their laird to ride through and lead them back to their respective keeps. And as the armies turned to ride back, there was a line of men who continued to face forward. They would remain in place until everyone was enough of a distance away that they would pose no threat.

Keithen knew it would be a long standoff as neither side would want to concede first and turn away.

His father motioned for him to ride alongside him and Keithen did so. "How is yer leg, Son?"

Knowing his father would say very little, Keithen didn't ask any questions. Instead, he motioned to his leg. "Not very much pain for my first ride."

It was half a day's ride back to their keep and by the time they arrived, Keithen could barely stand the pain. Sharp pains traveled down his leg and he required assistance dismounting. Once inside the great room, he refused to see the healer, who hurried toward him.

He hobbled to his father's study, where Broden, Ewan and several council members were already seated.

Despite the pain, Keithen did his best to keep from groaning out loud when he lowered to a chair.

"The Mackenzie expected that our alliance was intact. I told him different," his father stated. "I informed him that the attempt to hang my son dissolved any goodwill between us."

Keithen agreed. "What was the final outcome? Did ye tell

him about the attack on our guard?"

"Aye," his father replied. "I told him that we will not stand for attacks on our men on our lands and that if we find the attacker is a Mackenzie, I will not hesitate to order my men to kill any Mackenzies on our land."

"He became quite indignant at that point," Broden said. "He began accusing us of killing the last two Mackenzie lairds."

Neither Keithen nor Esme had told anyone that it was she who'd shot Alastair Mackenzie. Keithen had convinced his sister that he did not want Ava to know. She'd been through enough without having the added burden of knowing her husband's sister was responsible for her brother's death.

"It had to have been a Ross who killed Alastair. Clan Ross arrived before we did," Ewan said. "However, I must say, whoever the archer was who severed the rope, I would love to compete against him. That man had the best marksmanship I have ever seen." He shrugged. "Besides me."

Broden grunted. "That would be interesting." He met Keithen's gaze and he realized his friend was aware that Esme was the only archer with the ability to sever the rope at a long distance.

Ewan continued. "That same archer could have possibly shot Alastair and caused his death."

Keithen looked to his father, but the laird was listening to a council member asking a question.

"We ended the conversation with sort of an impasse. We will each stay away from the border until after winter. At that time, we will meet again."

The laird then looked to Broden. "How is yer guardsman?"

"He will recover," Broden informed them. "Now, Ewan and I must meet with the guard and ensure they are aware that they must stay away from the border lands. Also, I will send men out to inform the villagers and farmers who live near there."

Broden and Ewan had to help Keithen out to where the healer and Ava waited. He was half-carried to a small chamber where they examined his leg.

"It was not rebroken, but it is very bruised," the healer informed him. "Ye should not have gone. Tis too soon."

His leg was washed, wrapped and a new splint applied. He couldn't help groaning with each painful movement. It was almost a relief to take the tonic handed to him by Ava.

"Bring someone to help ye carry him upstairs," Ava said to a guard who stood at the door. "Hurry."

Once he was settled in bed, most of the pain was ebbing. "I do not require to lay down." Keithen said, sliding up to sit.

"What happened?" Ava asked lowering to a chair she'd dragged closer to the bed. "Did Atholl agree to keep peace?"

"For now. It will be revisited after winter." Keithen took her head. "I am proud of how well ye are handling the household."

Ava shrugged. "It is a daily struggle, actually. But I expected it."

"I can talk to the servants," Keithen replied.

"I would prefer ye did not."

He knew the news he was about to give her was not something she'd like to hear. But in a way, he hoped it would mean, in the end, things would turn out well.

"Prior to Mother's return, Esme and her husband will return. They plan to remain here for the winter."

It was clear by her expression that Ava fought not to show how upsetting the news was. "I was not aware."

"Hopefully, this will give ye and Esme an opportunity to come to some sort of a…" He wasn't sure what word to use.

"It is she who does not care for me. I have no ill will toward yer sister. Although, I agree that it is my fault for having caused what happened."

Keithen lifted her hand to his lips. "If I had not killed those guards, the Mackenzies would not have taken me and, well, the rest would have been avoided."

"I suppose we all have our share of blame. But it does no good. I will attempt to construct a cordial relationship with

Esme."

Despite his wishing to remain awake, the tonic began to take effect.

When Keithen woke, it was dark out and Ava was snuggled against him. Her soft breaths fanned warm air onto his shoulder, and he pressed a kiss to her temple.

It was hard to imagine life without her, which surprised him. He'd never thought to be the kind of man who would coddle his wife. But now, more than anything, he wanted to protect her. He desired to give Ava everything she desired. However, his wife proved to be self-sufficient and quite adept at doing things alone. She'd had plenty of practice not depending on anyone. The more he learned about the lack of caring by her family, the more he wanted to provide it for her.

He was grateful that his mother and Catriona had befriended Ava. If not for them, she would have no one to speak to and feel at ease with. Both his mother and Catriona felt they owed their lives to Ava and, because of it, they liked her.

The staff and his sister would be hurdles Ava had to traverse alone. He'd tried speaking to Esme, but his sister was headstrong. The servants could be dealt with. He'd ensure his mother punished those who'd been disrespectful to Ava.

For his part, he would care for his wife and ensure that she was aware he'd always be there for her.

A realization that he loved the woman with all his heart made him take a deep breath. He was in love with his wife.

By the time the sun rose, Keithen was already awake and dressed. He'd managed to slip from the bed without waking Ava. Now, he waited for her to wake so he could inform her of his feelings.

He'd never asked, but surely men informed women when their feelings changed.

"Why are ye staring at me like that?" Ava asked groggily. "Ye look angry."

Keithen attempted at a smile but failed when his stomach

tightened. "Nay. I am not angry."

"Oh." She yawned and stretched. "What is it then? Are ye in pain?"

His heart hammered, making Keithen wonder if something was, indeed, wrong. "I need to tell ye something."

Her eyes widened and she sat up. With her mussed hair and sleepy eyes, she was enticing. The tops of her breasts became exposed as the ribbon of her night rail had untied.

"Err," he stammered. "I must inform ye that I…well, ye see, I feel that…no, that is not right."

Ava narrowed her eyes. "Have ye taken tonic again this morn?" She slipped from the bed and came to him. "Come, I will help ye to sit."

Pressed against his side, she pulled his left arm over her shoulders. "Come along. Ye shouldn't be standing."

"I do not wish to sit." Keithen tried to push her away, but almost lost his balance and both of them swayed sideways.

"Keithen, if ye fall, yer leg could break again. Why are ye being so stubborn?" Ava snapped and took a step away. "What is the matter with ye this morning?"

He glared at her. "Last night, I woke up and ye were asleep."

This time, she looked toward the wardrobe. "Did I talk in my sleep?"

Keithen shook his head. "Ye did not. But I thought about ye and how independent ye are because ye had to be. How ye have never had a family like most. Ye know, like mine. One that cares for one another."

Clasping her hands against her chest, she turned away. "I did not have a caring family. What does that have to do with anything?"

"I want ye to know that I will always be yer family. I will always stand with ye."

Ava turned back to face him. The expression on her face was heartbreaking. It looked like she wasn't sure how to react. Something akin to sadness filled her eyes.

"That is the kindest thing anyone has ever said to me." Ava sniffed. "Thank ye."

Keithen motioned for her to come close, and she took hesitant steps until she arrived in his arms. His eyes fell shut as she wrapped her arms around his waist. "Ava, what I feel for ye, I have never felt before. I love ye, Wife, with all my heart."

When she gasped and looked up at him, there were tears in her eyes. "How can ye say that? I thought ye were in love with Catriona."

"She is very special to me. I love her like a sister. But what I feel for ye is much deeper. It fills me with the need to care for ye and ensure ye will always be safe. I wish to protect ye and to give ye anything ye desire."

He took her mouth, enjoying the familiarity of the beautiful woman's body against his.

Clinging to him, she let out a long sigh and placed her head on his chest. "I have felt the same way about ye for a long time."

There was a knock on the door and Keithen called for whoever it was to enter.

A maid stepped in and blushed at seeing them in an embrace. "I was told to inform ye that visitors arrive."

"Visitors?" Keithen went to the window and looked out. Outside, the morning haze made it hard to see clearly, but he made out the Ross banner.

"My sister and her husband are here."

Chapter Twenty-Two

THERE WERE STILL several hours until last meal and Ava wasn't sure what to do with her time. Just a few days after Esme arrived, Lady Fraser returned from her travels. That left Ava with nothing to do. Her garden was gone until spring and she could not spend time with the other women in the sitting room without it becoming awkward.

A couple times, she'd sought out Catriona, but Esme had been with her. She'd given up trying to seek out companionship, other than Keithen.

When her head bobbed from sleep, Ava put her embroidery to the side and went to peer out the window. Upon opening it, frigid air instantly brought relief from any sleepiness.

There were only a few people in the courtyard. Guardsmen gathered around a bonfire and several maids hurried to the well.

The men watched the women until one said something. They all laughed at whatever words were exchanged. Probably some sort of flirting.

"Ava?" Flora peered around the door. "I knocked, but ye didn't answer. May I come in?"

"Of course, please do." Ava hurried to pull a chair over for the woman. "I am glad to see ye."

Flora sat and smiled. "I needed to get away for a few moments and haven't seen ye much as of late."

"It is obvious Esme would prefer I not be around, so I'm keeping my distance." Ava sighed. "Unfortunately, it means I'm in here most of the day."

"Ye should speak to her."

"Do ye know her well?" Ava asked.

Flora shook her head. "No."

⁂

AT LAST MEAL, Ava kept her attention on the room and away from Lady Fraser and Esme, who discussed plans for the upcoming Yule celebration.

A maid came up and placed food between her and Keithen, who paid her no heed as he spoke to his father about a situation with two farmers.

The room buzzed with conversation, people laughed at whatever others said. At one table, a group of men began singing, and at another, women gathered, watching them.

In the center of it all, Ava felt adrift and lonely. Since all the guardsmen now ate inside, Catriona took her meals in her bedchamber, which meant Flora did as well.

"Taste the meat, it is very good," Keithen said, nudging her arm.

Thankful to be brought from her musings, Ava did as he asked and smiled at him. "It is quite delicious."

"I must speak to the patrol guards once the meal is over. I will come to our bedchamber once I am done," Keithen informed her as they finished the meal.

Ava was thankful to get away. As much as she hated spending so much time alone, it was preferable to being around people who would rather have nothing to do with her.

Deciding to go to the kitchen to fetch some warm cider, she

walked there and fetched a large cup and filled it from the liquid that was kept warm in a kettle that hung beside the fire.

Because she wasn't looking forward to returning upstairs, Ava hesitated when Eileen, the cook, walked in. "I could have served ye. All ye had to do was ask," the woman said, seeming off-put.

"Do not concern yerself with it. I did not mind." Ava went to pass the woman, but Eileen spoke and stopped her.

"May I ask ye something?"

"Yes, of course."

"Once, a long time ago, I tasted a delicious fig pudding." The woman lowered her voice. "It was a Mackenzie recipe. Would ye happen to know it?"

Ava nodded. "I believe so." She frowned. "Would it be horrible of me to share it?"

Eileen shook her head. "Tis not like they would find out about it."

"True," Ava said, enjoying prolonging the conversation. "I will think of it and try to remember what was in it and share it with ye."

"Thank ye." Eileen's chubby face beamed. "Enjoy the cider. I put honey in it."

Feeling better at making headway with the cook, Ava made her way to the stairwell. At the bottom of the stairs, she heard Keithen's voice followed by a woman's.

A tightness in her chest was followed by her stomach clenching. Why was her husband with a woman after telling her he was to meet with guards?

When she looked to the great room, there were a group of guards gathered at a table, speaking. None of them paid her any heed. Laird and Lady Fraser were gone, so were most of the other guests. Just one woman lingered at a table with a slumbering child in her arms.

It was best to find out what was going on. Ava was not about to continue to her bedchamber until she knew what her husband was doing.

She placed the cider on the bottom step and tiptoed around the side. Beside the stairwell, there was a short hallway with three steps down to a semi-hidden alcove.

It was easy to stand in the hallway without being seen, so Ava flattened against the wall and listened.

KEITHEN'S VOICE WAS first. "Ye need to stop acting so stubborn. I am as much to blame for what happened. There is no reason for her to know. What good would come of it?"

A hard lump formed in Ava's throat. He'd professed his love to her just a couple weeks earlier and now…

"I do not care one way or the other if she knows or not. I will not tell her, but if she finds out that I was the one who shot her brother, then so be it."

The woman was Esme. At first, Ava was relieved. But then at hearing what was said, she could barely breathe.

"She has gone through enough without having to find out her husband's sister killed her brother." Keithen sounded angry.

"I am sure he survived my shot. I ensured it." Esme huffed. "I saved yer life and all ye are concerned with is yer shrew of a wife. Whatever ye say, she is the cause of ye almost dying and, finally, her brother's death." Esme's loud voice carried clearly. "I will try to be nicer, but do not ask me to feel badly about her brother's death. He almost killed ye."

"I understand," Keithen replied.

A strange numbness filled Ava. There were no thoughts or feelings, just an emptiness that, in a way, was welcoming.

She walked back to the great room, grabbed a cloak from near the doorway and went outside. Once in the courtyard, she went to her horse's stall and dug in the back where she kept a bundle of clothes. She then guided the animal out and straight to the gates.

One of the guardsmen neared.

"Do ye require an escort?"

"No, I am walking about the keep with my horse. I do not plan to ride him."

The man shrugged. "Make sure ye stay where the guards can see ye."

In truth, she had no idea what to do. In the past, she'd run away when a situation became unbearable. This time, she wasn't sure if she wanted to get away or not. Keithen was fighting with his sister to protect her. To leave would be a betrayal to him.

She guided the horse along the front of the keep to one end and then back to the other. The docile horse, not at all upset at being out of the stall, enjoyed her attention.

"Ava," Keithen hobbled to her. "What are ye doing out here?"

Obviously, the guard had informed him, and he'd hurried out because all he was wearing was his tunic.

She stopped walking and studied his handsome face. He meant so much to her that she wanted to weep at his concerned expression.

"In the past, whenever I was upset, I ran away. I almost did it this time, but knowing ye would be hurt stopped me. For the first time in my life, I have a reason not to run."

Keithen walked to her and lifted her face. "Why did ye come out here?"

"I overheard ye and Esme speaking. She shot my brother."

"Aye, she did."

A frigid wind blew, and Ava shivered. "Her shot did not kill him right away. My brother would not allow healers to help and the wound festered."

"With everything that has happened between our clans, there will always be reasons for rifts. However, ye and I should not allow it to affect us."

Tears of frustration spilled down her cheeks. "Ye should have told me. There was no need to keep such a secret. Why did ye not tell me?"

Keithen let out a breath. "Because ye have been through

enough." He took the horse's reins from her frozen fingers. "Come inside, please. It is very cold."

Of course, he had to be chilled through without any protection from the wind. Ava allowed him to guide her and the horse back inside the courtyard.

A stable man rushed to them and took the horse away as she and Keithen continued inside.

Once inside, they walked up the stairs to the bedchamber.

Thankfully, a cheery fire burned in the hearth and they went to stand in front of it. Keithen met her gaze. "What did ye hear?"

Ava repeated what she'd overheard.

"After learning she was who'd severed the rope because of her keen skills, I wondered if she'd been the one to also shoot my brother. But there were so many archers there. I am shocked to know she could get so many shots off that close together."

"She is without compare. Even our head archer always lost against her in competition."

A thought went through her, too hard to bear. Ava closed her eyes. "Did she kill my father?"

Keithen came up behind her and wrapped his arms around her, pulling Ava against his chest. "No."

Sagging with relief, she stared into the flames. "I am not sure how to feel."

"Get some rest. We can discuss more in the morning, if ye wish. I hope that, eventually, ye and Esme will not be at odds."

She doubted they'd ever be cordial and certainly they'd never be friends, but Ava decided not to mention it to her husband. Alastair had died because he'd not accepted the truth of his injuries. If he'd lived, he would have never functioned properly as a man. Esme had known how to purposefully shoot him in a way to maim him forever.

It would be impossible to see her without thinking of what she'd done.

"From now on, we should be honest with each other," Keithen said, his fingers under her chin. He pressed a soft kiss to her lips. "Is there anything I should know?"

Ava shook her head. "No. I promise."

Once undressed and in the bed, she waited for Keithen to join her. He was a bit slower moving, but his leg was healing, and he moved about unaided now. According to the healer, it was possible he'd have a permanent limp.

A lifelong reminder of her actions. Being reckless and impulsive. Ava considered that if Keithen had died, then Esme was right to blame her.

Her actions had, indeed, caused everything.

Every instinct screamed at her to leave, to get away to somewhere where no one knew her and start over.

Then, Keithen's arm came around her waist and he pulled her close, her back against his chest. "Stop thinking. Everything will work out. Ye will see."

The glow from the fire lit the room enough that she could see. A sudden thought struck her. She'd left the bundle of clothes with the horse. If they were discovered, Keithen would know a truth about her that she'd not revealed. She should have burned the clothes. Her rebellious actions, riding out, and fighting against men, having saved Keithen a couple of times, was not something he would understand. No man wanted a wife who fought, wearing a mask and acting like some sort of renegade.

Then again, perhaps if he recalled her saving him, he'd not mind.

Ava let out a breath. In the morning, she'd retrieve the clothes and decide what to do.

THE SUN HAD barely risen when Ava hurried to the stables. She walked straight to her horse's stall and squeezed in, looking around. Her bundle of clothes was not there. She scrambled to recall the night before. She'd grabbed them before going outside the gates, which meant she could have dropped them while deciding what to do.

Pulling her cloak tight, she hurried toward the gates and

slipped out. There were several people already arriving from the village. It still struck her as strange that the clanspeople seemed to have no qualms visiting the laird on a regular basis.

She hurried along the wall, peering down, but did not see the clothes. Perhaps they'd been taken by someone on patrol.

Perhaps it was for the best. If the clothes were gone, there was no reason to tell Keithen about it since she had no plans to ever do any kind of sword fighting again. The only thing she'd kept was her sword, which was stored in her trunk. If it was ever found, she'd claim it had belonged to her father or brother.

"Is the Mackenzie woman still here?" a woman asked another as they ambled to the front door. The pair was not aware she was behind them.

Her companion huffed. "Aye, and from the looks of it, she has bewitched Keithen Fraser. Tis sickening."

Ava stopped walking, not wanting to be noticed by the women. Although she knew the clanspeople did not accept her, knowing and hearing it were two different things.

Following the flight of a bird, she tracked it until it disappeared. "Ye heard them."

The last person she wanted to speak to at the moment was Esme Ross. Ava kept her gaze on the horizon and shrugged. "Tis not as if I did not know how most people feel."

"Why did ye not go live with yer mother?"

"Because my mother left without telling me. My brother did not wish me to be there either." At this point, Ava's voice was loud. "My uncle would not allow me to remain unless Keithen was dead and then only if I married the new laird. Since my family killed my first husband and tried to kill Keithen, I wonder if the third would have survived unscathed."

When Esme's eyebrows shot up, and she started to say something, Ava cut her off.

"If given a choice of living elsewhere or being hated here, I would choose to remain here. I love my husband and he loves me. No matter what, I know he will always be there for me and I will die before I allow anything bad to happen to him."

Esme opened her mouth and Ava put a finger up. "No one else matters. Ye can continue to dislike me for causing what I did. There is nothing I can do about it."

She stormed inside, through the great room and up the steps. Once inside the bedchamber, she blew out a breath and clenched her hands into fists. Pacing from one side of the room to the other kept her from screaming with fury. Now she understood why Keithen did it. It helped.

"I found these," Esme said from the doorway.

Ava whirled to find Keithen's sister holding up the sack she'd been looking for.

"I have no idea what that is."

"I planned to give them to Keithen." Esme entered and put the sack down. "But it would be spiteful of me. He does not know, does he?"

Ava shook her head. "No. I planned to tell him."

"I would not, if it were me," Esme said and rolled her eyes. "My brother quite admires the man who has, on several occasions, interceded on his behalf. It could ruin the 'Masked Hero' image that the men have formed in their imaginations."

Despite not being comfortable with Esme, Ava considered what the woman said. "Why would ye care? Keithen would probably not believe it anyway."

"What would I not believe?" Keithen said, walking in and then moving directly to stand beside Ava. "Esme, what did ye do?"

Esme met Ava's gaze for a moment and then looked to Keithen. "That two women said hurtful things about Ava, and I chastised them for it. I told them if they continued to be disrespectful to our family, they'd not be welcome to return."

"My wife is right. I am not sure I believe it."

"Well, it is true," Esme said, glaring at Keithen. "Ava, I apologize for being less than civil to ye."

Ava nodded, her gaze moving to the sack on the floor next to

Esme.

Keithen's sister bent and lifted the bag. "I must be off to take these to the servants to launder. I plan to wear men's trews and a tunic for the archery competition."

Chapter Twenty-Three

Although it was cold, it hadn't snowed in days. It was a clear day and, yet, Keithen couldn't help but find the idea of an archery competition idiotic.

Only his sister and Ewan would consider it a good idea.

Thankfully, the splint on his leg had finally been removed. He'd been patient and waited as long as possible. Ava had insisted he keep it on and continuously inspected his leg.

He limped but, in his opinion, it wasn't as bad as he'd expected. His wife, however, considered it a horrible outcome and massaged the leg every night. Not that he minded, as sometimes the massages turned into bedsport.

"Are ye competing?" Esme asked, walking up to him with a grin. "The more who compete, the more I can beat."

Keithen could never beat his sister, yet the competition would be entertaining. "Why not?"

Keithen looked at Esme, contemplating his next words. "Esme," Keithen started. "What happened to change things? Ye invited Ava to the sitting room yesterday afternoon."

His sister pressed her lips together, considering what to say. "She has no one. I am fortunate to be able to come here and spend time with ye and our parents. Ava does not have any family to visit. Her mother prefers to keep her at arm's distance."

"True. She only has me. When ye are not here, Mother does spend time with her."

"That is not fair." Esme shook her head. "If I spend time with her around the clanspeople, they will be more accepting as well."

"Thank ye." Keithen pulled Esme to his side. "It will help."

His sister shrugged. "I cannot say I will ever care for her, but I do understand her."

The targets were set up and spaced apart as the next competition was about to begin. Of all the archers, there were only ten left to compete. Those who were eliminated stood on the sidelines watching. Some were placing bets, others were grumbling good-naturedly about the fairness of their elimination.

There was a festive atmosphere. Several bonfires warmed people who surrounded them. At a tent set up alongside where the archers were to stand, Keithen's parents and his aunt and uncle, who traveled there for the occasion, relaxed while they watched the competition. Ava, Catriona and Flora sat just behind them.

His father and uncle were having a grand time judging shots and choosing winners. They joked each time someone was eliminated, which brought laughter and ribbing between the competitors.

At the moment, his father pointed at one archer. "I hear yer wife complains about yer marksmanship as well."

Everyone laughed, including the archer who called back, "Her target is quite small." He smiled in the direction of his wife. "And I love it!"

The next contest was to be for speed. Only five archers were to compete, including Esme, Broden and Ewan. Each was given five arrows. Whoever emptied their quiver the fastest would win.

As the archers lined up, the crowd hushed until the only sounds were the crackling of the firewood and an occasional noise from the stables.

The aroma of roasting pig wafted through the air and Keithen hurried to stand next to Ava, who'd jumped to her feet to get a better view.

At the signal, the archers began to yank arrows with amazing speed, shooting one and then another into the target.

Keithen noted that Ewan only shot twice and lifted his arms in victory. Esme whirled around to face him, her eyes wide. "How did ye do that?"

Astonished murmurs filled the air. Everyone wanted to see Ewan demonstrate again what he'd just done.

Once again, five arrows were put into his quiver. Ewan made a show of setting up. Feet apart, he lifted the bow. Then as quick as lightning, he shot three arrows at the same time, and then two. The arrows formed almost a perfect circle on the target.

Everyone began to clap as he bowed, turning to face those gathered.

"That is amazing," Keithen said to Ava.

She'd turned white, her eyes wide and her mouth open.

"Ava? What is the matter?" Keithen took her arms and turned her to him. "Ye look like ye have seen the dead."

Pushing his hands away, she shook her head. "It's nothing. I just recalled something. I'm going to inform Eileen who won. She wishes to make them a tart." Turning from him, she walked toward the house.

"Did ye see that?" Esme approached Keithen. "Where is Ava going?"

"To the kitchen."

"He will have to teach me to do it." His sister grinned. "I got second place."

Keithen smiled at his sister. "Ye won the first one. Give someone else a chance in the distance one."

Shrugging, she went to speak to her parents.

Surrounded by archers, Ewan was enjoying the attention. Keithen went to congratulate him only to note that Broden stood aside with a pensive expression.

"Upset that ye have not won yet?" Keithen joked. "Perhaps ye can beat Esme in the distance contest."

Broden motioned for him to walk away from the group nearby. "Do ye know how the first Laird Mackenzie died?"

"Aye, shot with multiple arrows before anyone could intercept…" Keithen stopped talking and turned in the direction where Ewan was celebrating. "Do ye think?"

"The guards said there had to be more than one archer to get away with so many shots before they could react."

At the realization, he turned toward the house.

Ava had to know, which was why she'd reacted the way she had. After all, she'd been the one to help heal her father. How much more did his poor wife have to endure? Not only did Esme cause her brother's death, but now the man who killed her father lived in the same house.

"We will not know for sure unless we ask him," Keithen said. "Why would he kill Laird Mackenzie? It makes little sense. Ewan just recently moved to this region. As far as I know, Clan Ross had no qualms with the Mackenzie."

Broden gave him a knowing look. "There are circumstances that make a man do dangerous things." His friend motioned toward Ewan.

While accepting congratulations from his father and uncle for winning, Ewan kept turning in Catriona's direction, his gaze lingering on her before turning back to the laird.

"He'd only just arrived when Laird Mackenzie died. I doubt he'd even met Catriona then."

"It could be," Broden said, "there is another reason. Ye may want to speak to him and find out if what we suppose is true."

Someone called out for those competing to gather and Broden left. Keithen wasn't sure what to think. Even if Ewan was the man that shot the laird, whatever his reason, it didn't matter at this point.

A new laird was in place and life had continued. Perhaps Ava suspected that Ewan may have killed her father, however, there was no proof, other than him being an extraordinarily fast archer.

Just as he headed to the house, Ava emerged. She looked to him with a soft expression.

"The distance competition is about to begin," Keithen told her and held out a hand. "I am curious to see if Broden will beat Esme."

Ava took his hand and they headed toward the tent. "I am quite impressed by Esme. She is better than most of the men."

Her color had returned, and she seemed normal. As much as Keithen wanted to ask how she felt, it was best to wait until they were alone. "Esme has always been an outstanding archer. Her vision is clear and her hold is quite steady."

His wife nodded and then scanned the target practice area. There was a flicker, a slight narrowing of her eyes when looking to where Ewan took his place.

All was not well. Just as he'd thought, Ava was suspicious of Ewan.

AFTER A DAY of competition and feasting, Keithen was more than glad to have time alone with Ava in their bedchamber. He undressed and slipped into bed next to her and pulled his wife onto his chest.

"Did ye enjoy the day?"

She nodded. "I did. It was a good change. I believe we all needed a day outdoors."

"True. What about the competition?"

"It was very interesting. I am quite impressed with yer sister's skills. I wonder if she allowed Broden to win the distance exchange."

Keithen laughed. "No. Esme would not do that. He actually beat her."

They were silent for a moment and he continued forward. "Ewan's speed was very surprising. I was not aware he could do that."

"I do not think anyone did. It made the day more exciting."

Her lips pressed against his throat. "Ye know what else would make this day memorable?" She nibbled at his earlobe.

All thought evaporated when her hand slid down his stomach to between his legs and Keithen was immediately hard. "I am more than willing to make memories with ye."

"I want no clothing to come between us," Ava murmured, pulling her nightshift up and over her head.

Keithen quickly removed his long tunic and allowed her to push him back onto the bed.

The weight of her body over his was perfection. Under his palms, the silkiness of her skin made him clutch her against him, needing to feel every inch pressed together.

"Mmmm," Ava murmured against his ear as he cupped her bottom and lifted his hips to rub his shaft down the center of her sex.

Her apex was warmth and wetness, demanding to be taken, devoured by him. Keithen flipped Ava onto her back and moved down so he could taste her. Ava gasped when his mouth covered her sex, his tongue flicking the tiny engorged nub.

Needing more and wanting the sensation of her coming undone while his mouth took her, Keithen circled his tongue inside her lips as he slipped his finger into her wetness. Ava bucked and cried out and trembled.

The closer she neared to release, the more relentless he became in his efforts. He slipped his fingers in and out of her, suckled at her center and reached up with his other hand to run the pad of a finger over her tight nipple.

Ava screamed in release, her body going rigid before she went limp.

And still, he was not nearly done. Spreading her legs, he thrust into her and almost came undone when her tight sex wrapped around him.

The view of Ava, eyes closed, hair spread out like fire and her lips parted, was the most beautiful he'd ever seen. With every thrust, her gorgeous breasts bounced like ripe fruit demanding to be picked and eaten.

"Ahhh!" she cried out, once again shuddering with a second release and Keithen fought not to finish yet. He wanted to prolong the sensation by holding back.

"Keithen," Ava whimpered, her hands clutching his hips. "Faster."

Knowing it would be his undoing, he did as she demanded and thrust hard and fast. She met each of his drives, pushing back against him until losing control and flailing as she cried out for the third time.

Keithen's release was extreme, and he lost control. Once, twice and a third time, he continued to move, his body slapping against Ava's, the sounds filling the chamber. When he came, a hoarse cry from deep in his throat erupted.

Collapsing over Ava, he could not bear to move.

Seeming to know he had to remain still for a moment to gather his wits about him, Ava slid her hands up and down his back and pressed a kiss to his wet temple.

"The ending to a perfect day," she murmured.

Perhaps he'd been wrong, and Ava did not think or suspect Ewan of any wrongdoing. He frowned. It was a good thing as neither he nor Broden planned to bring up the subject with the Ross archer.

"I love ye," Ava whispered in his ear. "Because with ye, I will never again be alone."

Keithen flipped onto his back, then turned to his side to look at the beauty beside him. He caressed her face. "My family will be yers and I will always, always, be with ye. Never doubt it."

"I do have one doubt at the moment," Ava said and Keithen braced for what she'd say.

He let out a breath. "What do ye question?"

She made a circle with a finger on his chest. "I do not think ye will be able to make love to me again tonight."

Keithen laughed, then grabbed his wife's arms, pulling her face to face with him. "Give me yer hand."

Guiding it to his already hardening member, he waited for Ava's fingers to wrap around it. Her eyes widened.

"I will be more than ready for ye, Wife."

The End

About the Author

Most days USA Today Bestseller Hildie McQueen can be found in her overly tight leggings and green hoodie, holding a cup of British black tea while stalking her hunky lawn guy. Author of Medieval Highlander and American Historical romance, she writes something every reader can enjoy.

Hildie's favorite past-times are reader conventions, traveling, shopping and reading.

She resides in beautiful small town Georgia with her super-hero husband Kurt and three little doggies.

Visit her website at www.hildiemcqueen.com
Facebook: HildieMcQueen
Twitter: @HildieMcQueen
Instagram: hildiemcqueenwriter

www.ingramcontent.com/pod-product-compliance
Lightning Source LLC
Chambersburg PA
CBHW070344200726
48294CB00003B/784

* 9 7 8 1 9 6 1 2 7 5 2 3 2 *